MOSTLY MICHAEL

MOSTLY MICHAEL

Robert Kimmel Smith

Illustrated by Katherine Coville

Delacorte Press/New York

Published by
Delacorte Press
1 Dag Hammarskjold Plaza
New York, New York 10017

Text copyright © 1987 by Robert Kimmel Smith
Illustrations copyright © 1987 by Katherine Coville

Manufactured in the United States of America

First printing

Library of Congress Cataloging in Publication Data

Smith, Robert Kimmel [date of birth]
Mostly Michael.

Summary: Michael's diary reflects the ups and downs
of his eleventh year, as he copes with braces,
troublesome relatives, a little sister not yet potty-
trained, the school play, and a big spelling bee.
[1. Family life—Fiction.   2. Schools—Fiction.
3. Diaries.]   I. Coville, Katherine, ill.   II. Title.
PZ7.S65762Mo   1987   [Fic]
ISBN 0-385-29545-6
Library of Congress Catalog Card Number: 86-19618

For Joan

APRIL 19—FRIDAY

I am so mad at my Aunt Helene I could spit!

Here it is my eleventh birthday and what does she give me for a present? This dumb old diary! How stupid can you get? Aunt Helene is probably the cheapest woman in America. She must have gotten this diary for about a dollar.

If I really wanted to keep a diary, which I don't, I would want to start it on January 1, wouldn't I? That's my Aunt Helene. My mom says she is a nutcase who never grew up. Like today, when she came over for my family birthday party, Helene was wearing this ratty brown fur thing around her neck that was a real animal one time because it had feet with claws and a head. The head part had a mouth with teeth and eyes like brown marbles. Mindy took one look at this furry animal head that was around Aunt Helene's neck and she screamed her face off.

Aunt Helene brought along her two little brats, Robert and Rupert, who are five-year-old twins. They went up to my room while we were having birthday cake and threw my stuff all over. What a mess! When I went up there later and saw what Robert and Rupert had done, I started yelling and cursing them. Mom, Dad, and Aunt

Helene came flying upstairs to my room and there was more yelling. My dad yelled at me for cursing and Aunt Helene yelled at Robert and Rupert for being so disgusting and Mom yelled at Aunt Helene for not watching her kids. All that yelling made Mindy begin to cry because it scared her and then she got this look on her face which we all know what it means. So Mindy wet on my rug.

I hope I don't have another birthday like this for a hundred years.

APRIL 21—SUNDAY

I am not going to keep writing in this diary. The only reason I am writing this is to beat Mindy to it. She takes her stupid crayons and writes in all my books, including schoolbooks. One time she ruined my report on a trip to McDonald's I wrote for school. My report had a big picture of a hamburger on the cover that I pasted on. Mindy ate about half of it.

I might as well put down what happened at my real birthday party, which we had on Saturday afternoon. It was a bowling party. That was my mom's idea, not mine. I am the worst bowler in America, maybe in the world.

The other kids did so much better than me it was ridiculous. Nathaniel Robbins, who we all call Ned, bowled 87 one game. Steve Adolphus, who we call Dolf, had the highest game, 106. Libby Klein won the first game with a 77. My score in the first game was 12.

We went to the restaurant in back of the bowling alley after that and had the birthday cake my mom had brought along. The people in the restaurant were mostly older guys and girls and they looked at me and

laughed when I blew out the candles. I was so embarrassed I thought I would die. Then they laughed more
when my friends and Mom and Mindy sang "Happy
Birthday." I hate it when people pay too much attention to me.

Anyway, that's the last thing I'm going to write in this
stupid diary.

MAY 2—THURSDAY

I think I have figured out why I think a diary is dumb.
It is because of the word *diary*. When I was little that
word was one of my spelling demons. I always read the
word *diary* and said it *dairy*. Even now I can look at the
cover of this red book and I say "dairy" to myself sometimes. So this book reminds me of cream cheese, sour
cream, and yogurt, which I hate.

Sometimes I am a little weird.

MAY 3—FRIDAY

Today was a very exciting day in school. I don't like
school very much. Let me be honest, I really hate it a
lot. But today we learned we are putting on a play!

The play is called *Young Tom Edison* and it is about
the man who grew up to be a great inventor. I think he
invented the electric light.

I knew right away that I wanted to play the part of
Tom Edison because it is the best part in the play. I
could be a great actor, I know that. I am the best
reader-aloud we have in our class. Nancy Briskin is sec-
ond-best, but there is no way she could play Tom Edison unless she cuts off her braids.

So we all went to the auditorium and listened to Miss
Grandola, who everyone calls Miss Granola. She ex-

plained the whole play. Then she called us up and asked us which part we wanted to play. A whole bunch of boys wanted to play Tom Edison, me included. Libby Klein wanted that part also, but Miss Granola said she couldn't. Libby got mad and said it was sex discrimination, but Granola said Libby could try out for the part of Tom Edison's mother, which only made Libby madder.

I listened to the other guys read Tom Edison's part and they were terrible. I read the part really great when it was my turn. I remembered to holler out the words because people in the back row have to hear you too.

Miss Granola says she will post a cast list on the bulletin board soon, but I already know I am going to get the part of Tom.

MAY 4—SATURDAY

This was a horrible day and it isn't over yet.

We went to the dentist, Dr. Kulko. His waiting room is so boring. There is nothing to do except read magazines. Mindy had to go to the bathroom seventeen times while we were waiting, but she didn't make anything. She waited until she was in the car going back home.

Dr. Kulko says I have to get braces on my teeth. Mom says I have to also. I asked why do I have to. Dr. Kulko said my teeth were growing in crooked and I wouldn't be able to chew my food right. I said I would be careful and chew every bite ninety-seven times. You know who won that argument.

BRACES! I HATE IT! BRACES ARE DISGUSTING!

I sulked around all through dinner. I really wanted to

cry. I am so ugly-looking anyway, and now I will have railroad tracks over my teeth. Yuch!

Mom and Dad went out to a party at the Rosmans' house. They live way out in the country. Doreen was our baby-sitter again. I hate Doreen. She is a dumb fifteen-year-old girl who is ugly but thinks she is really gorgeous. She spends most of her time combing her long blond hair and using my mom's lipstick and makeup.

Doreen is sex mad. All she thinks about are boys. She calls up boys on the telephone and talks crazy. I am not kidding. I listen in on the telephone extension in the den. "Hello, sexy," she said tonight, "I am all alone and dying to see you." "Who is this?" the boy on the phone said. "The mysterious lady," Doreen said, "and I am hot stuff, big boy." It was so funny I started to laugh and Doreen hung up and came running after me and I had to lock myself in the bathroom until she calmed down.

MAY 5—SUNDAY

While I was in the bathroom I made goofy faces at myself in the mirror. Anyway, I got this idea when I found some paper clips. I kind of untwisted them and made them look like braces. Then I fitted them in my mouth so I could see in the mirror what those braces would look like. They look really ugly, which I knew anyway. But the thing of it was, I couldn't get them out. And while I was trying to untie them from my back teeth I scratched a hole in my gum, which hurt so much I started to yell, and also my mouth was bleeding.

Meanwhile, Doreen was banging on the door and trying to get in. I opened the door for her and she got so scared. Doreen was afraid I would swallow the paper

clips and die. When she said that I got even more scared and I started to cry. That woke up Mindy, who came into the bathroom, and she began to cry too. Finally, Doreen got the paper clips out of my mouth.

Just then Mom and Dad came in. We were making so much noise that we didn't even hear them come home. Mom was mad at me for being up so late, mad at Mindy for being out of bed, mad at Doreen for letting things "get so out of control." She was also mad at Dad for drinking too much at the Rosmans' party so when he said something she kept saying "Shut up, Henry."

Mom just came into my room and said to put out the light and stop writing in my diary. I reminded her about my Little League game tomorrow at nine o'clock. She said, "Forget about it," and I think maybe I better.

MAY 6—MONDAY

I am writing about what happened yesterday, Sunday, but I used that page already. This is my book and I can do what I want. Sometimes I am going to have to use more space when really important things happen. They make a diary with all these evenly spaced days, but a person's life is not like that. My life is very uneven. Days and days go by and nothing important happens. Then I get a day like Saturday and I could fill up a whole book.

Yesterday we went to a barbecue at Uncle Charlie and Aunt Madeline's house. Charlie is my dad's brother. He is very rich.

Mom hates Aunt Madeline. She thinks she is stuck-up and snooty. She also hates Uncle Charlie, I don't know why. I like their house, which is big and roomy. Charlie and Madeline are the only people I know who have a swimming pool. They also have three cars, a whole bunch of dogs, a maid, but no children. So when Mindy and me come over, which is not often, they always make a fuss over us. Except they really don't know how. Aunt Madeline is always asking me what I want to be when I grow up, which is maybe one of the dumbest things you can ask a kid.

How do I know what I will be when I grow up? I always say, "An adult, I hope," when somebody asks me that question. I do not want to be a cop or a fireman, which some kids do, because I do not want people shooting bullets at me and I don't want to run into burning buildings. I just know that I want to work at something that is not too hard to do or makes me work on the weekends, like Dad does. He is in the real estate business and he shows people houses on Saturday, and most times on Sunday too.

It was a very boring day, with nothing to do except run around chasing the dogs. It was not hot enough to swim in the pool. Mostly the adults sat around and talked and drank cocktails and talked and drank some more cocktails. Then Dad got into an argument with Charlie and we had to leave.

Some barbecue. There wasn't a hot dog or a hamburger in sight. Mom drove home and Dad fell asleep in the front seat. And that was another boring day in the story of my life.

MAY 7—TUESDAY

Mrs. DeBoer, who is our new language arts teacher this term, reminded us that we had to hand in our book reports in one month. I guess I had better find a book to read and report on. I looked through our school library, but I couldn't find a book that looked interesting. The book I read last term, *The Baseball Life of Johnny Bench*, was not there. I guess some other kid is going to write a report on it and has it at home.

I had better do something about a book soon.

MAY 8—WEDNESDAY

Steve Mayer said he wants the part of Tom Edison and I said so did I. "No chance," Steve said in his show-offy way, "you were awful in the tryout." I said I was better than he was, but he just laughed.

Steve Mayer is the smartest kid in our class, but he is not the nicest. He is always showing up other kids in class.

Steve has already handed in his book report, plus one more for extra credit. I think I hate him.

MAY 9—THURSDAY

Two strange things happened today.

Mom was sick this morning at breakfast. She was making soft-boiled eggs for Mindy when she got this funny look on her face and rushed to the sink and threw up. She sat down in a chair right after that and put a wet dish towel on her forehead.

Then, when I got home from school, there was an invitation to a party waiting for me. It was from a girl in school, Marcy Lipton, who is not even in my class. I mean, I hardly even know Marcy Lipton. So why did she invite me to her birthday party?

Mom was feeling better and she said she was pleased that I was being invited to Marcy's party. "It's very important to be popular," she told me. Now I'm sitting here in my room thinking about what she said. I don't think I am popular, like Mom said. And I don't think I am unpopular, either. I am someplace in the middle in my school in popularity, I guess. I am not the smartest kid in my class or the dumbest. I am not the best athlete or the worst. I am not the handsomest boy or the ugliest.

Call me Michael in the middle.

MAY 10—FRIDAY

Miss Granola was absent so the cast list was still not posted. Libby Klein said she was going to boycott the play. I told her I thought that was dumb. "If I get the part of Tom Edison," I said, "I would want you to play my mother." "You get the part of Tom Edison?" Libby said, then she began to laugh. She told me I was the worst one in the tryout, that I hollered so loud it made all the kids in the back of the auditorium laugh. "We all thought you were trying to be funny," she said.

"I wasn't," I said. "I thought I was really good."

"Well, you weren't," Libby said.

During lunch I sat with Ned and Dolf. They said I was awful too.

Why do I always fool myself this way? Why do I always think I have done great on a test and then find out I really didn't do too good? Because I do not always want to know the truth.

MAY 11—SATURDAY

Today we went to the Grandview Mall. This is a big shopping mall near where we live. I like going to the mall because we almost always get ice-cream cones at Steve's Ice Cream.

Mom was buying shoes for Mindy and some clothes for me. She wanted to buy me a jacket, she said, which I would wear to Marcy Lipton's party. "Wait a minute," I said, "I'm not going to Marcy Lipton's party."

Mom looked startled. "Why on earth not?" she asked.

"Because I hardly know Marcy Lipton," I said.

"Well," said Mom, "she knows you and she must like you."

"And I wouldn't know anyone at her party," I said.

"So what?" Mom said. "They'll all be kids like you. It will be fun. Parties are great. You get a chance to meet other kids and make friends."

"Why should I spend money for a present for a girl I hardly know?"

"Don't worry about it," Mom said. "I'll pay for the present, Michael, but I want you to go."

And then Mom went into her routine, which I have heard a million times, about how she thinks I don't have enough friends, that I spend too much time in my room alone, and it isn't healthy not to have friends.

She would probably have said more, like she always does, but just then she looked around and got this awful expression on her face. "Where is Mindy?" she said.

Mindy was lost, that's where she was. While Mom and I were arguing she'd just walked off.

We ran down the hall of the mall and back to the shoe store where we'd just been. No Mindy. So then we ran to Steve's Ice Cream, where we were sure Mindy would go, but she wasn't there. Mom was frantic by now, and we ran to the toy store, with Mom practically dragging me through the air she was running so fast. But she wasn't there, either.

"Maybe we should look for a trail of wetness on the ground and follow it," I said.

"That's not funny!" Mom practically screamed at me. I tried to tell her I wasn't being funny, I thought it was a good idea, but she wasn't listening.

We asked a security guard where the lost-and-found for kids is and he took us to an office. There was Mindy, sitting up on this counter, licking a lollipop. There was a puddle on top of the counter and a man was wiping it up with paper towels. He looked awfully mad. "Is this your kid?" he asked Mom.

Mom grabbed Mindy in a big hug and kissed her. "My baby," Mom said, and began to cry. Then, in the next second, she whacked Mindy on her bottom. "That's for running away!" she yelled at Mindy. "I told you *never, never* to do that."

"Look, lady," the man behind the counter said, "would you just get her out of here before she makes another mess?"

Then I told Mom I needed to do some shopping alone and she asked me why. "For tomorrow," I said.

"What's tomorrow?" she asked. I just looked at her. Tomorrow was Mother's Day, of course, but I wasn't about to say it to her.

"Oh," she said, then she smiled. We made up to meet at Steve's Ice Cream and I went off to the card store. I bought Mom a card that had flowers all over and a yuchy long poem about how wonderful a mother is. Mom has a pretty good sense of humor sometimes, but not about herself.

Then I bought her a coffee mug with her name on it, Sally. It cost $5, just about all the money I had. I only get 50 cents a week for my allowance, which is practically

nothing. Libby gets a dollar a week and Ned gets the same, but his grandma slips him another $1 a week that his parents don't know about. My folks are pretty cheap.

MAY 12—SUNDAY—MOTHER'S DAY

Weekends are different in my house because my dad goes to work most of the time. You would think that for an important day like this he would stay home, but he had to show a house this morning. At least he let Mom sleep late and he made breakfast for Mindy and me. He only knows how to cook French toast, so that's what we had. Then he had to go off, but he told us to let Mom sleep as much as she wanted and not to wake her.

When we heard the sound of water running in Mom's bathroom, Mindy ran upstairs and yelled, "Happy Mother's Day!" They came downstairs together and Mom was really happy about her coffee mug. And she loved the card, like I knew she would. She kissed me and gave me a hug and said I was her big boy and practically grown-up. That made me feel good, even though I knew it wasn't true. Then she kissed Mindy and hugged her and then called me over and gave us a family hug all together. "You children are the best thing in my life," she said, and started crying.

"What about Dad?" I asked.

"Him, too," Mom said, but she didn't sound like she meant it. In the afternoon, when Dad came home to take us all out to dinner in a restaurant, I noticed that Mom was not so lovey-dovey with him. She called him Henry, which is his name, but she usually calls him Hank, and even Hankus-Pankus when she is kidding around with him.

I sure hope they are not heading for a divorce, like Jimmy Rossillo's parents. I do not want to be a kid from a broken home.

MAY 15—WEDNESDAY

Everything is a mess.

I am so disgusted I do not even want to write it down. The cast list for *Tom Edison*—the dumbest play ever written—was posted on Monday. I did not get the part of young Tom Edison. Steve Mayer got it. I have one crummy line. "Tom Edison, that's disgusting and stupid!" That's all I say.

I hope the play is awful. I hope no one remembers their lines. I hope the scenery falls down. I hope the audience boos at the end. I hope Steve Mayer has to take off his eyeglasses onstage and bumps into the furniture.

I may never write in this diary again.

MAY 17—FRIDAY

Last night Mom made me call Marcy Lipton and say I was going to her party. This was the conversation.

ME: Hello, Marcy? It's Michael Marder.

MARCY: Hello.

ME: I'm coming to your party.

MARCY: Good.

ME: Bye, Marcy.

My mom was so mad. "Couldn't you say you were happy to go to her party? That you were looking forward to it?" she asked me.

"I am not happy to go to her stupid party and I am not looking forward to it," I said.

"She will think you have no manners," Mom said.

"I don't care," I said.

"Oh, Michael," Mom said, and she sighed.

And that was the end of another awful week of school. And I still don't have a book for my book report. And next week I go to the orthodontist to get braces.

MAY 19—SUNDAY

It was a boring and dumb weekend.

I spent Sunday afternoon looking into the mirror over my dresser. I think my nose is too long. My brown eyes are kind of squinty. I tried to look sideways to see my profile, but it was hard to do. So I kind of peeked out of the corner of my eyes while I was sideways. I looked like a goof that way. Also, my ears are too big. The only good thing about my face is my smile. And now I am going to have railroad tracks all over my teeth.

If I was a dog, they would shoot me for ugliness.

MAY 20—MONDAY

I did not think my life could get worse, but today it did.

We are doing a project on farming and Miss Fishman made up committees to write reports on farm produce. First of all, I hate Miss Fishman, who everyone calls Fishlips because she holds her mouth kind of pushed together like a kissing gourami. Fishlips would not let us choose our own committees so we could be working with friends. No, that makes too much sense. So she put us into groups and gave out assignments. "It will do us good to work with new people," said Fishlips, "because maybe we can all make new friends." She sounds like my mother.

Here is my committee: Linda Dawson, the fattest girl

in school and a complete idiot, and Jimmy Rossillo, who doesn't care about anything since his parents got divorced.

Our subject is "Beans, the Secret Protein."

YAAAAAHHHHH!

MAY 22—WEDNESDAY

We had our first play rehearsal in school today. We all have to memorize our parts by next week. Steve Mayer, who has the biggest part of all, has it memorized already.

I went to the library to look for a book for my book report. Every book I picked up looked so boring, or else they were for girls.

Here is what I want in a book. First of all, a short one. Or a funny one with lots of jokes. It should be for boys and about boys. Or on a subject boys are interested in, like baseball.

The Baseball Life of Johnny Bench was still not there.

MAY 24—FRIDAY

The name of my orthodontist is Dr. Hertz. They named him right. He hurts.

First, he put these pieces of cardboard in my mouth and took a whole bunch of X rays. Those cardboard things had sharp edges, and when he pushed my jaws together they pinched me a lot.

But that was not the worst part.

He explained to me how he had to make a mold of my teeth and jaws. To make the mold he had to put this pillowy pink stuff in my mouth and have me bite on it. It tasted disgusting, like the worst kind of bubble gum that also makes your mouth dry. I thought I would throw up when he shoved all this rubbery stuff into my mouth. Then I was afraid it would all go down my throat and choke me.

It took about half an hour and not one part of it was fun.

That's the bad news. There is no good news.

MAY 25—SATURDAY

Two things happened today. First, Mom went potty crazy, then I went to Marcy Lipton's party.

Mindy wet in the kitchen in the morning. Mom hit her on the butt, then began to cry. "You are impossible!" she yelled. Mindy was crying too.

Later, Mom called her friend, Laura Drager. Laura said if Mindy could make number two in the potty, she could make number one in it also if she really wanted to. I agreed with Laura. I can never understand how Mindy has good control of herself for one thing but can't manage to do the other in the right place.

So Mom brought the potty down from Mindy's room, and Laura came over with two more potties, and they set up potties all over the place. Then they watched Mindy like crazy and kept slapping her down on one potty after another all afternoon. But nothing happened. Except that later, when Laura was going home and Mom was outside saying good-bye, Mindy made a big puddle in the kitchen.

Mom made me get dressed really neat for Marcy's party. It was a dinner party, starting at six o'clock.

I felt really nervous walking into Marcy's house. But her mother seemed nice, and Marcy said, "Hello," and I said, "Happy birthday," and then we went downstairs into the basement, where all the kids were, and I saw that Jimmy Rossillo from my class was there. Later on, Libby Klein walked in so I had at least two people to talk to.

Marcy Lipton is a plain kind of girl. She has a nice smile, though, and brown hair that sort of drapes over her eye on one side. I told her I was kind of surprised to be invited to her party because we don't know each other very well, and Marcy laughed and said I was invited for a special reason. When I asked her what was the reason she only said, "You'll see."

The food was very good. Marcy's dad made hamburgers on the grill in the backyard.

Later we went back down to the basement and danced to some music. I don't know how to dance, but I kind of jumped around like everybody else, mostly with Libby Klein. I told Libby about Marcy's mysterious invitation and she looked at me like I was an idiot. "Don't you know why you're here, birdbrain?" is what she said.

"No," I said.

"One of Marcy's friends is very lovey-dovey about you," Libby said. "She thinks you are really cute."

"Who is it?" I asked. "What's her name?"

"That would be telling," Libby said, and she danced away from me.

I found out the truth later, when we were playing a really stupid game called "Love Mates." All of our names were put into two bowls and Marcy pulled out a boy's name from one and a girl's name from the other and the two kids whose names were called got to go into the bathroom together for two minutes. When they came out the girls all asked stupid questions of the kids. Like, what color is the boy's eyes, they would ask

the girl. And, is she a good kisser, they would ask the boy.

The funny part was nobody got to see the names of the kids who were paired up except Marcy. I got suspicious when she didn't even look at the names she was supposed to be reading. Then she called my name. All the girls started to giggle so much I couldn't even hear the name of the girl Marcy called out. But I knew her from school, she was in Marcy's class. Her name is Carrie White. She is short and has blond hair and blue eyes and she took my hand and kind of pulled me into the bathroom behind her, then locked the door.

"Your name is Carrie, isn't it?" I said.

Carrie nodded. Actually, she is not a bad-looking girl, with pink shiny skin and a pretty mouth that was even a brighter pink. "And you are my special Michael," Carrie said in a sort of whisper.

Then she reached out and turned the lights off.

"What'd you do that for?" I asked.

"It's more romantic this way," she said.

I was thinking this was very dumb, but I didn't say it.

"You can kiss me now," Carrie said.

"Kiss you?" I said. "I hardly know you."

"That doesn't matter," Carrie said. She put her hands up behind my head and pulled it down toward her face. The next second we were nose-to-nose. Before I could move away Carrie was pulling my head forward and we kissed for what seemed an hour but was probably only a minute.

"Please, Michael," said Carrie, "put your arms around me."

I did. I really didn't want to very much, but I didn't

want to hurt Carrie's feelings by not doing it. So we stood there in a hug for a while and it wasn't too bad.

Then everybody outside started yelling "Two minutes." We opened the door and went out. Well, everyone was laughing and pointing at me and it didn't take too long for me to figure out that I had Carrie's pink lipstick all over my mouth.

I pulled out my handkerchief and wiped my mouth like crazy. Then Carrie and me sat down together in a corner and talked for a while. She said she fell in love with me in the fall and she wanted to talk to me but was always too shy. And it was Marcy who made up the game so that we could get together in the bathroom.

"So it was a frame-up," I said, which is what I thought.

Carrie nodded. "Yes," she said. "Are you mad at me for that?"

"I don't know yet," I said, "I'll have to think about it."

MAY 27—MONDAY—
MEMORIAL DAY OBSERVED

Today my dad was home all day. Dr. Schaeffer was having a barbecue for all the neighbors in his big backyard. Mom was making potato salad. She skinned a whole bunch of potatoes after she boiled them in a big pot. They were still steaming hot while she peeled them and she was saying "Ooh" and "Oh" and "Yikes" because they were burning her hands. We both began to laugh because it was funny.

Before we went over to the Schaeffers' house, Mom and Dad got into a big argument. It had something to do with Uncle Charlie. They both started yelling and said some nasty things and I couldn't stand it and walked out onto the front porch.

The party was okay. The best part was that I met a new kid who just moved in down the block. His name is Brian Beam and he is about my age. He goes to Gracemore Academy, which is a private school. His father is a doctor.

Brian and me kind of hung out together during the party. He has no brothers or sisters.

It's getting late and I can't stay up too much more writing this. But I've been wondering about Mom and Dad. How could two people who have been married for thirteen years and are supposed to be in love be so mean to each other? I would never even say to Mindy what they said to each other, because in spite of how much she annoys me and acts so stupid and bad she is still my sister.

I don't understand what's going on in my house.

MAY 29—WEDNESDAY

Fishlips broke us into our committees today and we sat together all during class. Linda and Jimmy didn't say much, so I saw that I had better take charge or else there wouldn't be any report to hand in. I asked who was the best artist because I knew for sure I wasn't. When I draw a person it looks like a gorilla. Jimmy said he could draw, so he will do the illustrations in our report. Linda said she had a good encyclopedia at home so we made up to meet at her house. I said I would make the outline and do a lot of the writing. Then Jimmy said he knew a poem about beans that maybe we could use to start our report. "This is how it goes," he said.

"Beans, beans,
The musical fruit,
The more you eat,
The more you toot."

I don't think we'll use it.

MAY 30—THURSDAY—TRADITIONAL
MEMORIAL DAY

We had our first rehearsal of *Young Tom Edison* today and it was terrible. Nobody knew their parts except a few kids, including me because I have only one line. Libby is the stage manager of the play. This is a mistake.

I like Libby a lot. She is one of my best friends in school. But she is so bossy, like a dictator. She was screaming at us today the minute we did something wrong. I think she called seventeen kids "birdbrain"— which she says a lot.

Steve Mayer not only knows his own part, which is the biggest, but he knows everybody else's part too.

His brain must be awesome.

MAY 31—FRIDAY

Miss DeBoer told us we have one more week to hand in our book reports and I am nowhere close to even picking out a book yet. What I do know is that I am about to do something bad. I know this and I am still going to do it.

I am kind of surprised at myself.

I have always been a scared kind of kid. When a teacher or Mom says do something, I mostly do it. I figure grown-ups are the bosses. And when I grow up I will boss little kids and show them the right way.

I still have last term's book report that I handed in to

Mrs. Gruen. Mrs. Gruen moved away and does not teach in our school anymore. I got an "A" on that report last term and I want to get an "A" again.

Miss DeBoer will never know that I am using the same book report twice. My mom would know, but I am not going to show it to her.

I am scared about doing this, but not scared enough.

JUNE 2—SUNDAY

It's funny how I always end up writing so much on Sunday night. Maybe because a lot happens and I have more time to think about it.

Carrie has been my shadow all this week. She kept sitting with me in the lunchroom. She waited for me outside of school even though we could walk only two blocks together before she turned off to go home.

Libby says that Carrie always has a boyfriend for one term and then gets another one. She says not to worry about it.

BOYFRIEND?

The funny part is that I don't mind being with Carrie. She is kind of quiet. She looks pretty. But I don't know her well enough to have a big conversation with her. I could talk more with Libby than with Carrie. And I never for a minute would think about Libby as my girlfriend.

I like Libby as a friend. She is smart and funny and brave in a way I am not. So why would I want to spoil that with lovey-dovey stuff?

Now I am laughing. I can just see myself asking Libby to be my girlfriend. I can hear her saying, "What are you, stupid, you birdbrain?"

JUNE 4—TUESDAY

Our Bean Committee got together after school at Linda's house.

Linda's mother is even fatter than Linda! And her older brother looks about as big as a house. It was a great place for a meeting if you like to eat. Linda's mom served us ice cream and homemade cookies that were terrific. And while we worked we nibbled on candy, pretzels, chips, and soda. In between the eating and the nibbling we worked a little.

All the stuff we need for our report is in Linda's encyclopedia. Including some pictures and illustrations on how beans grow and other stuff that Jimmy says he will draw. I agreed to write the report and Linda will copy it neatly because my handwriting is awful.

It was the first time that Jimmy and me ever got to spend time together, and he is pretty nice. He has changed a lot since his parents got divorced two years ago. He was in my class back then and he was a funny guy, always laughing and joking around. He is much quieter now. I would be his friend if he wanted.

JUNE 5—WEDNESDAY

Tonight I got out my last term's book report on *The Baseball Life of Johnny Bench*. Then I took fresh paper and copied it over again. It looks really neat. I will hand it in to Miss DeBoer on Friday.

Why am I doing this? It wouldn't have been so hard to find a new book. But I never really looked hard enough. And I think I knew I was going to do it when I started looking for the Johnny Bench book in the library. I knew it then but I wouldn't think it out loud to myself.

You are weird, Michael Marder.

JUNE 7—FRIDAY

I am getting a little annoyed at Carrie. Like today, when we were having lunch. I really wanted to be with Libby, Dolf, and Ned. But Carrie sat down and there were only two seats left near me and my whole bunch went and sat someplace else.

It bothered me, but I didn't say anything.

In class with Miss DeBoer we had to write a character sketch of someone we know really well. Here is what I wrote:

"My little sister, Mindy, is a strange person. She is three and a half years old and she is only halfway toilet-trained.

"Mostly, I like her, but she can be a pest. When she was a baby she was so cute. She would grab my finger and squeeze it and I could make a funny face at her and she would make this dopey grin with no teeth in it.

"I remember how we would sometimes lie on Mom's bed, Mom and me and Mindy, and we would have fun. I could play peek-a-boo with Mindy all day long and she would still want more.

"It was great when she learned to say my name. She called me Mike-oo. In the morning I would hear her in her crib calling, 'Mike-oo, Mike-oo.' And when I went into her room she was so excited she would start jumping up and down. I know she loves me a lot and I love her, too, but not so much lately. As soon as she started to walk around she began coming in my room and messing up my stuff. Also, she throws temper tantrums and yells and screams a lot. Mom says this is a phase and she will quit it sometime soon.

"So this is my sister, Mindy Sue Marder. She can make you laugh in a minute, but she can also make you want to scream."

At the end of the period I handed in my book report on *The Baseball Life of Johnny Bench.*

Now I am a criminal.

JUNE 8—SATURDAY

Carrie called this morning. When Mom handed me the telephone she looked funny. Carrie wanted to come over and spend the afternoon. I told her no. I really didn't have a lot to do, just going shopping for a Father's Day present with Mom, but I didn't want Carrie hanging around.

The reason Mom looked funny was because Carrie said she was my girlfriend. To my *mom,* she said this.

So then Mom asked me about her. I told Mom all about the party at Marcy Lipton's house, and how Carrie has been my shadow ever since.

"Do you want a girlfriend?" Mom asked me.

"No."

"So what are you going to do about it?"

"I don't know."

"Maybe you ought to have a talk with this Carrie and tell her," Mom said. "In a nice way, of course. You must never hurt anyone who loves you, Michael, but you should be honest with them too."

"I'll think about it," I said.

And I will.

JUNE 9—SUNDAY

Dad was going off to work again so he was making breakfast for Mindy and me. "You're always working," I said. "It's unfair."

After that I told Dad that I didn't ever get to see him anymore, which is true. My mom even calls him "the mystery man" once in a while. So I said I wanted to go to work with him today. He said no, of course, but I decided to be like Mindy when she wants something. Dad said he had to show three houses today and I would get in the way, but I said I would be so good it would be amazing. I guess he liked the way I said that because he grinned and said okay.

Dad's office is in a little shopping center off the highway. On the window it says HANDAL & MARDER, Real Estate Brokers. Sam Handal is Dad's partner. There is this big room out front, with a few desks and some chairs for people who are waiting. In the back there are two private offices and one of them is Dad's.

So I hung around with him all day and it was great. Sometimes it was a little boring, but I was amazingly good, like I said.

My dad is big, about six feet two, and I think he could still pick me up with one hand like he used to. He is always wearing a shirt and tie and looks neat. He uses this after-shave that has an interesting smell, and he always uses a mouthwash that smells like mint.

In the morning we went with this couple to see a big house. Later on, Dad took me to lunch at a nice restaurant that had green plants everywhere and shiny white tablecloths. People were eating brunch, but we got lunch menus. Dad ordered a vodka on the rocks and I had a ginger ale while we studied the menus. I don't know why I took so long reading the menu because I knew I was going to have a hamburger anyway.

Dad gave the waiter our orders and also asked for another vodka. When the waiter left I asked if he always had two drinks at lunch.

Dad looked at me and laughed. "You sound like your mother," he said.

"Also," I said, "you two are fighting a lot, I notice."

The waiter came back with Dad's vodka and he took a drink of it. We sat for a bit, not saying anything, then Dad reached over and put his hand on mine. His hand was cold from the drink, and a little damp. "Michael," he said, "your mom is under a lot of strain right now, and I guess I am too. But we love each other, and that's the important thing. It will all work out, you'll see, but in the meantime I don't want you worrying yourself about us, okay?"

"Sure," I said. "But I hate it when you two fight. It scares me."

"Poor Mike," Dad said.

"You could stop fighting," I said, "that'd be good."

"Sure would," Dad said. "Just hang on," he said, "this too shall pass."

I sure hope so.

JUNE 11—TUESDAY

We had a good rehearsal of *Young Tom Medicine*, which is what we are calling the play now. Everybody seems to know their lines, except a few kids still make mistakes or forget.

It's funny how Steve Mayer knows everyone's part. He has this scene with Lisa, and when she forgot her lines Steve just said them himself and then went on and said his *own* lines like nothing happened.

He could probably do the whole play himself, whipping on all the different costumes as he said the lines.

On the other hand, he would look funny in a dress.

JUNE 12—WEDNESDAY

Carrie was so annoying today. We were walking in the hall after lunch and I was talking baseball with Dolf, but Carrie was hanging on to my arm and yanking on it. So I interrupted my conversation with Dolf and turned around to her and yelled, "WHAT?"—real loud.

"I wanted to tell you," she said, "I love your shirt."

My shirt? Is that stupid, or what?

"Is that a reason to butt in when I am talking to Dolf?" I said to her.

Dolf started to laugh. "It's LOVE!" Dolf said real loud, and then he put his hand over his heart and pretended to faint and he made goo-goo eyes at me and Carrie. So other kids began laughing and I was the center of attention and I was mad at Dolf for doing it and embarrassed as anything.

Carrie has to go.

JUNE 14—FRIDAY—FLAG DAY

Well, diary, we are in a lot of trouble.

I first heard about it in the lunchroom when I passed Steve Mayer and his friends. "Miss Boring has something to tell you," Steve said as I was going to join Libby and Ned.

Steve mostly hangs around with Billy Alston. "Blam, blam," Billy said, "you are going to be shot down in flames."

"The Baseball Life of Johnny Bench," Steve said. "Naughty, naughty."

Well, of course I couldn't eat my lunch. If Steve knew about what I did then everybody in the school must know because Steve Mayer has a big mouth. So Miss DeBoer knows I handed in the same book report twice. How did she find out? Did Steve Mayer tell her? If he did, I'll kill him.

I told Libby and Ned about it. "Oh, no!" is what Libby said. "Michael Marder, how could you be so stupid?"

"I think you're in big trouble," Ned said, which I already knew.

The whole afternoon was real torture. I sat through math class hardly paying attention. Then we went to Miss DeBoer's room. She handed back all the book reports so we could read them aloud in class. When she passed me she bent over and said, "I want to see you after class." And she didn't give me back my report.

I got all warm and sweaty then and I felt sick to my stomach. I sat and listened to the other kids reading their book reports. I was thinking about my mom coming to school, about the kind of punishment I would get. That was the worrying part. But underneath was this feeling of horrible shame.

Miss DeBoer was like an icicle when we spoke after class. She told me how disappointed she was in me. How could a smart boy and a good boy like you do something like this? she wanted to know. I had no answer for her, no answer she would like, anyway. Because I knew the truth.

I did it because I thought I could get away with it.

She made me stand there, staring at my toes, while she wrote a note for Mom and sealed it in an envelope. I

took the note from her and we looked at each other, then I looked down at the floor again. If there was a crack in the tiles I would have crawled into it. "Wouldn't it have been better to hand in a bad report, Michael, than to do what you've done?" she said.

I nodded.

"Cheating is not the way, Michael," she said. "It's your character that's involved here, not just a book report. Do you understand that?"

"Yes," I mumbled.

"I want you to go home," she said, "and think about what you've done. Next week I'll see you and your parents together."

That's about as low as I ever want to feel.

As I left school Carrie was waiting for me, but I didn't say one word to her while we walked the two blocks till she had to turn off for home.

I think Mom was harder to face than Miss DeBoer. She read the note when I gave it to her and I saw her cheeks go red. "Oh, Michael," she said, "how could you do such an awful thing?"

I didn't say anything. I just started to cry.

"I want you to go upstairs to your room and stay there until dinner," Mom said.

I turned away and ran up to my room. Mindy was awake after her nap and she saw me run by and throw myself on my bed. After a few minutes she came in. "Don't cry, Mikey," she said, and her little hand began patting my head where I had buried it in my pillow.

"I'm bad," I said, "go away."

"You a good boy, Mikey," Mindy said, "you my good boy." And she began kissing and hugging me to make me feel better. The funny part was it only made me feel worse. But after a while I stopped crying and Mindy snuggled up next to me and I put my arms around her in a hug. There was probably only one person in the world who was on my side now and here she was, in my arms and pressed against my heart.

JUNE 15—SATURDAY

How do I get into these troubles?

I've been thinking a lot about that, dear diary.

Last night I got a lecture from Dad about honesty and cheating. I got a million dirty looks from Mom. I cannot watch TV or play my stereo in my room until this is over. So I did have a lot of time to think last night.

I think I can be a real wise guy if I let myself.

Sometimes I get the feeling that I am smarter than Dad and Mom and the outside world. That feeling is really weird because there are other times when I feel so dumb. But I really felt that Miss DeBoer was new in the school and not too smart about us kids and that I could fool her.

That's enough for now. The master criminal has to go to sleep.

JUNE 16—SUNDAY—FATHER'S DAY

Mom got up and let Dad sleep late for once. We had juice and milk and waited to eat all together. When Dad came down later, dressed for business (he works even on Father's Day!) we gave him his present, which is a shirt and tie Mom helped me pick out and helped pay for too. He liked them. And he liked the card a lot.

Later on he went to the office, but he would not take me with him. I could not watch the baseball game on TV in the afternoon, so it was boring.

I asked Mom for permission to ride my bike and she said okay. I went around the block a few times and then set out for Carrie's house.

I rang the bell and her mother came to the door, then called Carrie outside.

"Look," I told her when her mother went away, "right now I do not want a girlfriend."

"Oh, Michael," Carrie said.

"First of all," I said, "I think it was sneaky to get Marcy Lipton to invite me to her party and to make up that game so you and me would end up in the bathroom together."

"Half of it was Marcy's idea," Carrie said.

"Whatever," I said. "But I figured out that having friends is more important to me than having a girl-friend who only wants me all to herself. It's not any-thing to do with you, exactly. I mean, you're very nice. And if I really wanted a girlfriend maybe it would even be you. But I don't."

"Why not?" Carrie said.

"I just told you," I said. "I don't have time for you."

"Is this about your book report?" Carrie said.

I was disgusted and getting mad. "You're not listen-ing to me!" I practically shouted at her. "I am *not* your boyfriend."

What Carrie did next just amazed me. She actually smiled.

"It's our first lover's quarrel, Michael," she said like she was glad of it, "and I forgive you." Then she batted her eyelashes at me and smiled again.

"I give up," I said. I got back on my bike. "You are my

ex-girlfriend, just remember that," I shouted back at her as I pedaled away.

I don't think she got the message.

JUNE 17—MONDAY

Usually the first day of the last week of school before summer makes me so happy I think I'm going to bust. But not today.

I spent last night alone in my room, without TV or stereo. Just like I did on Saturday night. So I wrote the entire bean report in those two nights instead. I gave it to Linda to copy over really neat, and she gave the encyclopedia to Jimmy Rossillo so he could do illustrations.

That was the best part of my day. The worst was at the end, when Mom and Mindy came to school. First, Mom and Miss DeBoer had a long talk in her room while I waited in the hall with Mindy. Then they called me in. Mom took Mindy on her lap. Miss DeBoer talked to me for a few minutes that seemed like an hour. I would pass language arts, she said, but with the lowest mark she could give me. My work, except for the cheating book report, was excellent, and I even showed great promise in writing.

But I had to see Miss DeBoer after school on Thursday, when she would give me a further punishment. I think she would have said more but Mom interrupted by suddenly saying "OOH!" and jumping up with Mindy in her arms. Mom's khaki skirt had a big round wet spot all over her lap. Well, Mom was embarrassed and Miss DeBoer was smiling, and come to think of it, I was smiling too. We got out of school real fast and Mom was madder at Mindy than at me.

My kid sister is terrific.

JUNE 18—TUESDAY

After school Mom took me to see Dr. Hertz. She left Mindy with Laura Drager.

It was pretty bad, but not horrible.

Dr. Hertz put railroad tracks on my top teeth. And all kinds of wire went around them. And next week I have to go back because he is going to do more.

When I came out of Dr. Hertz's office Mom was waiting. "Smile," she said.

"I don't feel like smiling," I said. But I gave her a smile anyway.

"Not too bad," she said in her cheery way that is almost always phony. I knew she was only saying that to make me feel better. I had already seen how I looked because Dr. Hertz had shown me in a mirror.

How I looked was like Mr. Ironmouth, like railroad-track city, like ugly.

Here's the worst part. I have to wear these braces for two years!

I showed them to Mindy when we picked her up on the way home. "Ooh," she said, "they pretty, Mikey." What a dopey kid.

Dad was late for dinner and we didn't wait for him. Mom served some kind of meat and little pieces of it stuck in my braces. And I don't think I can talk straight anymore. My tongue kind of gets caught in the braces so when I say "yes" it comes out "yesh."

Dad said they looked okay and not ugly and that I

shouldn't worry about them. When they come off, he said, you'll have a great smile and straight teeth.

In the meantime, I am ugly. And on Thursday I get my punishment. I am very depressed.

JUNE 19—WEDNESDAY

I had a hard time falling asleep last night. My tongue kept going to the back of my teeth and feeling the braces. I tried to stop doing it and I couldn't.

We handed in our report on "Beans, The Secret Protein." It was very good.

All the kids were pretty nice about my railroad tracks. Libby said I looked no more ugly than usual. Dolf called me Metalmouth all day. Ned called me Tracks. Jimmy Rossillo said I was lucky, because he has tracks on the top of his mouth and the bottom.

Carrie thought they looked good. She is as dopey as Mindy.

Now I am going to sleep. I will not let my tongue touch my braces. I will not think about tomorrow, either.

JUNE 20—THURSDAY—FIRST DAY OF SUMMER

Tomorrow is the last day of school, but I may not live through it.

We did the play in the afternoon. Everybody kept on forgetting their lines, except for Steve Mayer, who kind of whispered the next line to whoever forgot.

But the worst was me. Finally, when it came to my line, here's what I said: "Tom Edi-Shun, thatsh dishgushting and thtupid!" It got a very big laugh that went on and on and Steve Mayer had to wait to say his next line. I was so embarrassed.

But Miss Granola said I was very good and that I should do my line the same way tomorrow when the parents are here.

Everybody had a good feeling because we had our first performance and it wasn't too bad. But I felt so scared all day, thinking about Miss DeBoer and my punishment.

I went to see her when school ended. She talked for a while about how surprised and disappointed she was in me. "What do you think of yourself?" she asked me.

"Not much," I said. "I think I did something stupid that made me worry a lot and maybe it would have been easier to write a book report."

"Much easier," she said.

"So it was really dumb," I said.

"If you've learned that, Michael," she said, "then you've learned a lot."

Then she handed me my punishment. It was a long reading list with maybe a hundred names of books and authors on it. I have to read ten of them over the summer and write reports on them.

Ten books! Ten book reports!

I didn't say anything, but I was really mad. The summer is when we go to the beach and go on vacation and I get to relax and have a good time. The summer is the best part of the year, and now it will be spoiled.

I should have told Miss Boring one more thing I learned. Crime does not pay.

JUNE 21—FRIDAY

Last day of school. Wow, yippee, hooray and hoop-dedoo!

My report card was okay, but I got a "D" in language arts.

The play went much better today. It was even good, although it is a stupid play.

The end of the play was the end of school for the year. So we were all saying good-bye backstage and afterward on the way home. Ned Robbins was crying. He has to go to this terrible place called Camp Lean-Too for the summer. He says they starve you there. It is all because Ned is really fat. A lot of kids call him Jelly Belly, including sometimes me.

Dolf was sad because he will go to Camp Sha-Kah-Na-Kee all alone, instead of with Ned.

But Libby will be around, and the new kid on the block, Brian Beam, and a few other kids. Not that I will get to play with them. Ten books, ten book reports!

I will probably not set foot outside my room all summer.

JUNE 22—SATURDAY

The first day of freedom.

In the morning I got my first really good news in ages and ages. Grandma is coming to spend some time with us! Grandma is the best. She is terrific.

In the afternoon I looked over the reading list Miss Boring gave me. I'd heard of a few books on the list because some of the kids made book reports on them. I marked a check mark next to some that I remembered sounded good. That was only about four of them. Thinking about how much reading I have to do, I felt really depressed.

It is going to be a long, terrible summer.

JUNE 23—SUNDAY

Aunt Helene and Robert and Rupert came over after lunch. While I was saying hello to Aunt Helene the twins ran inside the house and right up to my room. I ran up there as fast as I could and stayed there, watching while they took all my old toys out of my closet and scattered them across my room. I told them they could play with any toys they liked, but not to keep taking stuff out and dropping it all over. Did they listen? You know they didn't.

Then Mom came up and said we should go outside and play under the lawn sprinkler. I said, "Let's go, guys!" and charged down the stairs and outside. I was wearing a bathing suit and a T-shirt. I threw off my T-shirt and ran under the cold sprinkler. When I looked around Robert and Rupert were naked and doing the same! And back across the lawn were all their clothes. And they stayed that way, all day long! It was really disgusting. And Aunt Helene didn't seem to notice that her kids weren't wearing any clothes.

My mom is right. Aunt Helene has some strange ideas.

JUNE 26—WEDNESDAY

I went back to Dr. Hertz for the rest of my railroad tracks today. He put them on and then added all kinds of wires and rubber bands, and he showed me how to put on new rubber bands when I break them.

And then I got this night brace.

It is like a collar that goes around my neck when I sleep and hooks up to the braces in my mouth. Dr. Hertz said I should also wear it in the day when I am just hanging around. And I have to keep going back to have my mouth checked.

I looked at myself in the mirror in the bathroom while I was wearing my night brace. I look like a kid from outer space.

Yuch!

JUNE 28—FRIDAY

Libby came over on her bike and we hung around together. We played catch in the driveway and then basketball, one-on-one, until we got too hot and tired. Mom made us iced tea and we sat on the back porch. I showed Libby my book list and she made check marks on the books she'd read and liked. They looked like mostly girls' books, but Libby said they were not.

I told Libby I will have to get a library card and she was surprised that I didn't already have one. "You mean you've never been to our library on Cortelyou Road?" she asked me. I said no and Libby sort of shook her head. We made a date to go there together next week.

JUNE 30—SUNDAY

What a good feeling it is for it to be Sunday night and no school tomorrow. I love the summer, even if it is boring. Because I really think that summer should be boring. It is one of the nice things about summer, the long empty hours with nothing to do but hang around. I can listen to my stereo or the radio or watch a ball game on TV at night and stay up really late. I can ride my bike or shoot baskets in the driveway or go to the beach with Mom and Mindy.

Or I can just do nothing and it is all the same.

I wish it was summer all year round.

JULY 2—TUESDAY

The day got off to a bad start when Mom was feeling nauseous after she made us breakfast. She sat down at the table and I could see she was ready to cry. "Michael," she said after a while, "I would like you to help me more around the house."

So she showed me how to clear the table and scrape off the plates and put them in the dishwasher. From now on that is one of my jobs, just like taking out the garbage, which I have been doing for a year already. Mom was happy then, but she got sad again when Mindy wet her pants. Mom started yelling and calling her a bad girl, and then she scooped her up and took her upstairs to her dressing stand.

I had watched Mom do this so many times that I said I would do it. Mindy wears these plastic diapers and it's easy as can be. I just took off the wet diaper, sprinkled on some baby powder, and put on a dry one. The diaper closes with this sticky tape, but Mindy stays nice and quiet so it is easy.

"You know what?" Mom said to me. "You just got the job. From now on you can change your sister when she wets."

"Okay," I said, and then I had a thought. "But not if she makes number two in her diaper. I won't go near that."

"She doesn't do that anymore," Mom said.

"But if she does," I said, "I won't clean it up."

"Deal," Mom said, and stuck out her hand, and I said, "Deal," and we shook hands on it.

It was good to see Mom smiling again.

JULY 3—WEDNESDAY

After lunch I met Libby at her house and we rode our bikes to the library. Libby introduced me to her friend, a lady with tall blond hair. Her name is Stacy. She is the children's librarian. Stacy typed out a library card for me while Libby went off to look for books for herself. I will have to get Mom to sign my library card, Stacy said, but in the meantime I could take out two books. After that, I could take out *ten books* if I wanted!

I showed Stacy my book list and she asked me what kind of books I liked. Easy ones, I said, because I am a slow reader. She smiled at that. "You know," she said, "if you keep reading you'll get better at it, and faster."

Stacy circled the names of some books on the list and showed me how they are arranged on the shelves. I got two books from my list and found Libby and we went home.

Now all I have to do is start reading.

JULY 4—THURSDAY—INDEPENDENCE DAY

I don't really want to think too much about this, but I have to put it down. I still can't believe it.

My mom is going to have a baby!

Dad was home for once, because it is a holiday, and after breakfast we sat at the table in the kitchen. "I have something to tell you kids," Mom said. She will have a baby sometime next January. And Mindy and me will have a little brother or a sister.

I didn't know what to say, and I was a little embarrassed by the whole thing. But Mindy piped up right away and said, "Where is the baby? I want to see the baby." So Mom told her it would be a long time yet

before the baby came to our house, and that Mindy should be patient and wait.

"What do you think, Michael?" Dad asked me.

"Great," I said, mostly because I think Dad wanted me to say that.

But I don't really know if it is so great or not.

JULY 7—SUNDAY

Well, now everyone knows about the baby.

Mom has been on the phone all weekend, telling all her friends and all our relatives. Grandma was so excited on the telephone. "You are going to be a brother!" she said to me.

"I already am a brother," I said.

"A new baby," she said, "so small and cute and cuddly. Maybe it will be a boy."

"That would be good," I said.

I remember when Mom was pregnant with Mindy. I was a little afraid of having a sister back then, or even a brother. Everybody was telling me how wonderful it was going to be when the baby was born and all, but I didn't believe it. I liked our house and our life back then, and I knew that a new baby would change everything. And it did. I don't like sudden changes too much.

But Mindy turned out all right, even if she does wet all over the place. So maybe the new baby will be okay.

But if my parents had asked me about having a new baby, I think I would have said we could do without it.

JULY 9—TUESDAY

I got to know Brian Beam today. He is more than a year older than me and bigger too.

Brian lives in the big house on the corner. Part of it is

his father's office. Right now Brian's dad is in Spain on a doctors' meeting with his mother. So Brian is at home alone with their housekeeper, a lady named Annie.

Brian's house is much bigger than ours and his room is huge! He even has his own bathroom with a neat stall shower. We watched some dumb game shows on TV and made funny remarks about them. Then Annie made us tuna-fish sandwiches and milk and cookies.

In the afternoon we played a really great game in Brian's dad's office. It was hockey. Brian got these flat wooden sticks called tongue depressors and they were our hockey sticks. We used a quarter as our puck and shot it back and forth in this small hallway. It was fun.

I think Brian is probably a little lonely. He is an only child, and with his parents away, he needs a friend.

JULY 10—WEDNESDAY

Grandma is coming next week!

She called this morning and spoke to Mom. Grandma lives in Toledo, Ohio, and she works in a hospital as a volunteer. She said she can't stay with us too long because her friends in the hospital would miss her.

She can stay in our house all summer, as far as I am concerned.

JULY 11—THURSDAY

My mouth started bleeding during the night and it was sore when I woke up this morning. One of the wires in my braces came loose and was hurting me. So we went over to Dr. Hertz's office and he put his fingers in my mouth and fixed it. I asked him if this was going to happen a lot and he just shrugged and said, "I sure hope not."

That didn't give me a good feeling, exactly.

I played at Brian's house again. I think Brian is a little weird. He started talking about crotch hairs and how his are all grown in already. Like a big deal, he opened his zipper and showed me his hair. Then he wanted to see mine. I don't have any yet, so I said I wouldn't.

So he started to tease me about it. He was really obnoxious, calling me a baby. I got mad and said he was a sex fiend and then I went home.

JULY 12—FRIDAY

I am sad and depressed.

I am disgusted with myself.

I am a stupid kid who won't ever amount to anything.

Libby called today and wanted to go to the library to return her books. She took out six books last week and finished them all. I have not even started to read my two measly books yet. She called me a birdbrain for not getting down to reading my books. She is right. I look at those two books sitting on my desk and I think, tomorrow I will begin the first one.

But I would rather watch a stupid ball game on TV. Or turn on my radio and listen to some music. Or flip my baseball cards across the room and try to land them in my wastebasket. Or take these dice and throw them and play baseball by the numbers that come up. Or ride my bike around and around the block a million times.

I really am a birdbrain.

JULY 14—SUNDAY

Dear diary, I have decided that maybe I am not such a bad person after all. Here are my reasons:

1) My parents love me
2) Mindy and Grandma love me
3) I love all of the above
4) I have friends I like and they like me
5) I don't cheat or curse too much
5a) I have to explain that I cheated on the math test only because I saw Libby's answer was right and mine was wrong. And I copied someone else's homework only twice all year. I will think about the cursing some more. I do it only when I get mad.
6) I have hit only three people in my life. Mindy because she ate my report, and I didn't hit her hard enough to hurt her. Jimmy Rossillo in the third grade when he stole my hat and wouldn't give it back. Phil Steinkraus because he deserved it.

My best reason is that I finally read book number one today. The book was about a Little League baseball team that was so terrible they never won a game. I started the book after breakfast and read it all day and finished it in bed a while ago.

It wasn't the best book I ever read, but it wasn't the worst.

JULY 15—MONDAY

Today I wrote a book report on the first book and read fifty pages of the second book.

The second book is good. It's about these kids who have a bet about eating worms. I don't believe it, exactly, but it's funny.

The best part of the day was when Mindy was napping and Mom was too and I sat in the shade on the back porch and read the book. In the book there is a barn and I thought about being in the country.

Would I be the same kid if I was the son of a farmer? Would I be the same Michael Marder if we had cows and chickens and grew corn? I know my *life* would be different, but would I be the same inside me?

Will I be the same kid after Mom has her baby?

No way, José.

JULY 17—WEDNESDAY

Finished the second book yesterday so I went to the library today and returned the two books. Stacy sat down with me and we had a really good talk. She asked if I was going to read only easy books, boys' books, and baseball books all the time. "Maybe you should think about branching out?" is what she said.

"Not yet," is what I said.

So I took out five books this time. I am sure three of them are good, and I will see about the others.

When I got home Mom was on the telephone with Grandma. She is coming next Monday, when the airfares are lower.

I started my third book, but still have to write my report on the second book. That part has always been easy for me, the writing part. I am good at putting my ideas down on paper. It's the reading part that makes me crazy.

JULY 19—FRIDAY

It was time to see Dr. Gilner today for my yearly checkup. He is a nice guy and he knows me since I was a baby. When I walked into his office he was out in the waiting room talking to a woman and he looked at me and said, "Is that Michael Marder, this great big almost-grown-up kid?"

I went into an examining room with Mom and stripped down to my underpants. I got weighed and then measured and examined all over.

Dr. Gilner makes a lot of corny jokes while he is poking and prodding and putting that cold stethoscope on me. Like, why does an elephant have a trunk? Because he doesn't have a glove compartment.

I asked Dr. Gilner if I was going to get a shot today. "Why," he said, "do you really want one?"

"No," I said.

"Then we'll just skip it."

That made me feel good. I hate shots and needles.

Dr. Gilner pulled down my underpants and looked at me. "When will I have hair there?" I asked him.

"Why," he said, "are you getting married soon?"

"No," I said, "I just want to know."

"You will get it when it grows in," he said. "Some boys get it at your age—just a few—and some boys don't develop until they are fourteen. Everybody has his own time."

That answered something I had been thinking about. Now I won't worry about it. Not until I am fourteen years old, at least.

JULY 20—SATURDAY

Mom had a lot to do today and we went all over the place with her. She is getting ready for Grandma's visit. Grandma is a vegetarian, so we had to get lots of foods like granola and whole-wheat spaghetti and bunches of different fruits and vegetables.

Mom aired the guest room and made the bed and fixed things up a lot. She seemed worried and I asked her about it. "She's my mother, Michael," Mom said, "and she's also like an inspector. So I want the house spotless for Monday."

In the afternoon Mindy saw me reading and wanted me to read *The Cat in the Hat* to her. I have done this only ninety-eight million times. Instead, I took Mindy on my lap and read my book to her. The book is about a kid in the fourth grade who has a little brother much worse than Mindy. After a while Mindy fell asleep and I carried her into her room and put her to sleep in her crib. As soon as I laid her down she closed her eyes and cuddled up to Horsie, her teddy bear. She looked so cute and beautiful lying there asleep that I just stood there a while, watching her.

I take back what I said about her being a dimwit.

JULY 21—SUNDAY

I think Brian Beam is a creep.

Today his parents were off playing golf. So he came over this afternoon and we played a game of Strato-Matic Baseball. Mindy wanted to play, too, but we wouldn't let her. She got loud and was yelling and then she wet her pants.

I took her upstairs to change her. Brian followed me and made some remarks I did not like at all.

I was embarrassed and sore at him, but I kept quiet. I just finished the diapering fast and got out of there. After that I didn't have much to say to Brian and he went home.

Brian is a sex fiend. I will never go in his house again,

that's for sure. And I will play with him only when he comes over.

I hope I won't be like him when I am his age.

JULY 22—MONDAY

Today we just kept moving all day long. Mom went and bought fresh flowers and put them in the guest room for Grandma. Grandma's plane was on time and we waited at the gate. The minute I saw her I started yelling, "Over here! Grandma!" She came running and we kissed and hugged and she did the same to Mindy and Mom.

Grandma is a small lady, maybe five feet tall, with gray hair and blue eyes. She is skinny and lively and moves fast. We collected her bags and went home. On the way Grandma gave Mindy this little doll with a red face and she had a present for me too. It was a T-shirt from the Toledo Mudhens, the baseball team from her hometown.

When Grandma unpacked she brought lots of food down to the kitchen. She brewed a big pot of tea made from something strange and when I tasted it, it was yuchy. I must have made a face because Grandma said I had to drink it all up. "It is good for your heart and liver," she said. I sipped it from time to time and hoped she wouldn't notice that I was leaving most of it.

"Now tell me about you and Henry," she said to Mom. "Are you still fighting like cats and dogs?"

"*Mother!*" Mom said in an embarrassed way.

"We can talk in front of the kids," said Grandma.

"I'd prefer we didn't," Mom said.

"Henry was right, you know, not wanting to go into business with his brother. He doesn't get along with

Charlie and never will. And no amount of money is worth all that aggravation."

Mom's face was as red as Mindy's new doll. "Mother, please!" she said.

"You were dead wrong, you know," said Grandma. "Money isn't everything, Sally. Being happy is more important."

"Let's not discuss it," Mom said. She got up from the table and walked over to the sink, turning her back on Grandma.

Now I knew what Mom and Dad were arguing about. Something about Mom wanting Dad to go into business with Uncle Charlie and Dad not agreeing. In a way I was happy to find that out. I was glad they weren't fighting about other things, like maybe not loving each other anymore, or even a divorce.

Dinner was strange tonight because it was two dinners. Mom made us meat loaf and potatoes, while Grandma cooked her own stuff. She had a salad with funny things in it and noodles with a sort of dark brown sauce that smelled awful. When I asked her about it she said there were apples, cranberries, and nuts in it. And all through dinner Grandma was pointing out what was wrong with meat loaf. She said it had cholesterol and that if we ate enough of it our hearts would "seize up and quit beating altogether."

It didn't make dinner taste better.

Then when Mom poured coffee she started in on caffeine and how dangerous a drug it was. I saw that Dad was annoyed. "Now, Estelle," he said to Grandma, "not everyone is cut out to be a vegetarian, so please let me drink my coffee in peace." And then he went on to say how Grandma had lived sixty-five years before she turned to health foods, and maybe we ought to be allowed to do the same.

Well, Grandma settled down after that. And after dinner she played dominoes with Mindy and me until it was time for Mindy to go off to sleep. That's when Grandma started talking about how Mom should have toilet trained Mindy by now.

"If you don't rule your children," Grandma said, "they will rule you."

Mom looked like she was going to scream, but she answered quietly. "I've tried everything," she said. "But Mindy has a mind and a bottom all her own."

"Not to worry," said Grandma. "I will have her trained in two days."

JULY 24—WEDNESDAY

I wrote my second and third book reports today. Grandma went off to see Aunt Helene and the twins. When she got back we talked about Mindy. She wanted to know what Mindy really liked for a treat. "Piggyback rides," I told her, "and watermelon for dessert."

"What about snacks?" asked Grandma. "Chips? Lollipops?"

"Chocolate," I said. "She's a fiend for chocolate. Especially those wafers with the little white dots on top."

"Ahah!"

She rounded up Mindy and we went off to the candy shop on Cortelyou Road. "We're here to buy chocolate for Mindy," Grandma announced when we walked into the shop. She picked Mindy up and showed her the nonpareils.

"Want them," Mindy said, "want them NOW!" She was real excited.

"A pound of your best chocolate nonpareils," Grandma told the man behind the counter. And when she got the bag she bent down to show them to Mindy. "These are only for you," she told her. "Nobody else is going to have any chocolate, only Mindy."

"Want chocolate," Mindy said when we got outside.

"When we get home," Grandma announced, "and not before."

Well, Mindy started crying like a baby, which she is. "NO CHOCOLATE if you don't STOP CRYING," Grandma said in Mindy's face. And Mindy shut up in about two seconds.

It was amazing.

When we got inside the house Mindy started jumping up and down and yelling, "Chocolate! Give Mindy chocolate!"

Grandma took the bag of chocolate and put Mindy on her lap, then practically put Mindy's nose in the bag. But she didn't give her any. "If you go to the potty and make something in it," said Grandma, "then Grandma will give Mindy chocolate."

Mindy was off Grandma's lap like a shot and ran to the potty. Grandma ran after her, pulled down her shorts and diaper, and put her on. I could see Mindy make her funny face and then she tinkled in the potty.

You would have thought Mindy had just won the Olympic marathon by the way Grandma jumped up and down and hollered. She picked Mindy up and gave her a big kiss. "Now Mindy gets chocolate all for herself!" Grandma announced.

We went back into the living room and Grandma gave Mindy one nonpareil. In about a minute it was gone. "Want more chocolate," Mindy said.

"Yes," said Grandma, as calm as could be. "When Mindy makes tinkle in the potty." Then she folded her arms across her chest and stared Mindy square in the eye.

I could see Mindy thinking about this. I could almost hear the little wheels going around in her head. I thought she would throw herself on the floor and start screaming her face off. But she didn't.

She turned around and ran off to the potty again.

Grandma looked at me and winked, and I thought that Grandma was like a superhero in her way. Nobody messes with Grandma.

JULY 25—THURSDAY

Today was just like yesterday. Mindy stayed dry yesterday, and Grandma told her she would get *two* nonpareils if she stayed dry all night. This morning I heard Mindy calling when I woke up. "Potty," she was yelling, "got to go potty."

I took her out of her crib and Mindy went off and did it on the potty. Then she went into the guest room and woke up Grandma, who got out of bed, inspected Mindy's crib, and gave her *three* nonpareils as a reward.

And Mindy stayed dry all day. By the afternoon she wasn't even wearing a diaper anymore!

Mom was a little ashamed of how Grandma had tricked Mindy. When she spoke up about it at dinner Grandma argued with her. "You do what works," Grandma said. "With the new baby coming you can't have *two* in diapers, Sally."

"And is this how I get Mindy to behave in the future? By bribery?"

"Bribery-shmibery," Grandma said.

"I still think it's wrong," Mom said.

"Is that so?" Grandma said with a smile on her face. "If it wasn't for jelly beans and lemon drops, *you* wouldn't have been toilet trained until you got married."

Mom didn't say anything more about it after that.

JULY 26—FRIDAY

Today I finished reading my fourth book and wrote a book report on it.

Only six more to go.

JULY 28—SUNDAY

I am writing less but enjoying life more since Grandma came. I stay up late with her and we talk and stuff and I get to bed too late to write much.

Grandma is great.

She told me all about Mom when she was a little kid. And how she was so ugly she made Grandma cry sometimes thinking she would look like that all her life. Mom had ears that stuck out, like me, and had squinty eyes just like me. And her nose, Grandma said, she despaired for her long nose.

But Mom changed almost completely when she was a teenager. By the time she graduated from high school, Grandma said, Mom was a real beauty.

So maybe there is hope for me. Maybe my face will change when I get a little older. Maybe, someday, I will even be handsome.

When I said that to Grandma she laughed and gave me a hug. "Kiddo," she whispered in my ear, "you are going to be a killer-diller!"

JULY 30—TUESDAY

Grandma made dinner for everyone tonight. Of course it was a vegetarian dinner, but Grandma said we would all like it.

First there was a crazy salad. It had lettuce in it, but a whole lot of other things too. There was this hairy stuff Grandma said was alfalfa sprouts. And there were all kinds of seeds and nuts and beans.

Then we had spaghetti, but instead of tomato sauce there was some kind of white creamy sauce and lots of vegetables. On top, Grandma melted pizza cheese. It was really very tasty and good. "If this is being a vegetarian, I could be one," I said to Grandma.

"Meat is evil," Grandma said, which sounded crazy to me. "It stirs up the blood and makes you mean."

"Wait a minute," I said. "You mean if I eat a hamburger I'll turn into a killer?"

Mom and Dad laughed at that, but Grandma answered me. "I mean the whole system of killing animals for food is wrong. What gives man the right to slaughter poor defenseless animals?"

"Man takes what he needs for food," Dad said. "Man always has."

"And just look at the world," Grandma said. "Wars, pestilence, famine, and poverty."

"You mean," I said, "if we just ate fruits and nuts and vegetables, we would be better people?"

"That's exactly what I mean," Grandma said with a smile. "Michael understands me."

"In that case," I said, "I'll have a double helping of your apple pie, Grandma."

JULY 31—WEDNESDAY

Libby came over and brought me some books to read. She is going away with her family for the whole month of August.

I will miss her a lot.

She brought me a book to read that is one of her very favorites. "This is a girl's book," I said.

"No, it's not," said Libby.

"Is it about this girl?" I asked, pointing at the girl on the cover.

"Yes," said Libby, "but it is also about her family and her friends in school."

"Then it's a girl's book," I said. "I won't like it."

"Don't be stupid," Libby said. "Just because a book has a heroine instead of a hero doesn't mean it's a girl's book."

"It usually does," I said.

"How about *Alice in Wonderland?*" Libby said. "Wasn't that about a girl?"

"Yes," I said, "but there were lots of other people and animals in it."

"Trust me," Libby said. "I wouldn't give you a bad book."

I took the book from her and we rode our bikes back to Libby's house and said good-bye.

So I will put the book on my reading list. If I don't like it, I will call Libby a birdbrain for once.

AUGUST 1—THURSDAY

I got a postcard from Carrie today. There was a picture of a cannon on the front and it was from Williamsburg, Virginia. Here is what Carrie wrote on the back.

"Dear Michael,
This is a nice place. It's all from Revolutionary times. The weather has been sunny and hot. I miss you a lot."

And she signed it, "Your girlfriend, Carrie."
She is so stupid! I told her a million times that I am not her boyfriend.

I got mad at Mom for reading my postcard before I did. The mail is supposed to be private. A person could go to jail for taking another person's mail.

AUGUST 2—FRIDAY

It rained all day today. It was a little boring just hanging around. I read another book and wrote one more report.

Only five more to go. I am halfway finished!

The book was the one that Libby gave me. I was right about it, but so was Libby. It is really a girl's book, but it is good for boys too.

I wrote a letter to Carrie. I will mail it to her house so she gets it when she comes home from vacation.

This is what I put in the letter.

Dear Carrie,
Please pay attention to what I write in this letter because I really mean it.

I am not your boyfriend.

I have never been your boyfriend.

I will never be your boyfriend.

Please do not ever call me your boyfriend again, or say I am your boyfriend to anybody else, or especially not write it to me in a postcard other people, including my Mother, can see.

Yours,
Michael Marder

P.S. We can be friends if you like, but that's all!

AUGUST 3—SATURDAY

Mindy has been dry for more than a week. She goes to the potty by herself and can even pull her own pants up and down!

This is amazing.

A long time ago Mom promised Mindy her own grown-up bed if she could be toilet trained. So today we went to the furniture store in the mall to buy a bed for Mindy.

Mindy ran around the store jumping on all the kids beds. Then she pretended to fall asleep on them.

Mindy liked a real expensive bed, but Mom wouldn't buy it. Mindy made a big fuss and I had to take her to Steve's for an ice-cream cone. She dripped it all over her playsuit, but it made her forget about the bed. Mom ordered one and it will be delivered to the house next week.

2:35 A.M.

Woke up from sleep and could not fall asleep again. So here I am, dear diary, passing the time until I get sleepy by writing.

Getting up in the night used to happen to me when I was nine. I worried a lot about it back then, but Mom told me I could put my light on and do things instead of just lying in bed like a lump and trying to fall back asleep. Once I started doing that, I didn't worry about not sleeping anymore.

I wish Dad was home more than he is. I don't know any other fathers who have to work on Saturday and Sunday like he does. It makes me lonely for him. Sometimes he takes a day off during the week, but I am usually in school then and I get to see him only when I come home.

3:46

I spent the last hour looking through my baseball cards and making All-Star teams. I think maybe I am sleepy enough to turn off my light and try to doze off again.

4:05

I was wrong.

I have been thinking about the new baby. I hope it is a boy. I will be eleven and three quarters when he is born. When he is six I will be almost eighteen. I will be able to teach him how to throw and catch a ball. I can teach him to ride a bike. When he is my age I will be twenty-two!

I can't imagine what I will be like at age twenty-two. I will be shaving, I will be graduated from high school and maybe from college! I will maybe even have a girlfriend.

I just thought of something. When I am twenty-two Mindy will be about sixteen!

This is too confusing. I just can't think of me and Mindy being grown-up yet.

AUGUST 4—SUNDAY

This was a lost day for me.

I slept until 11:30! That is my all-time record for sleeping late. When I got up, washed, and dressed and went down for breakfast, everybody was ready for lunch.

"Good afternoon," Mom said.

"We'd given you up for dead," Grandma said.

Even though I had slept so late, I was still tired. In the afternoon I plopped myself in front of the TV and watched the ball game. After that I went outside and lay down in the hammock and looked up at the pine tree. The next thing I knew, Mindy was waking me for dinner.

I went to sleep at nine o'clock.

AUGUST 5—MONDAY

Mom was wearing a different kind of dress today. The top of it was long and came down to her hips. Under that she wore pants. I can see her stomach is getting big.

I returned my books to the library in the afternoon. There were two books I had not read. I tried to, but I didn't like them. I told Stacy about the girl's book Libby had lent me and how I liked it. Well, it turns out there are three more books about this girl. I borrowed two of them that were in the library, and Stacy picked out two more books she thinks I will like. Neither one is about baseball.

I have only about a month left of vacation and five books to go.

AUGUST 6—TUESDAY

Mindy's bed was delivered this morning. The men brought it up to her room. Then the men put Mindy's crib in the attic. Mindy's new bed is as big as mine.

Mindy thinks her bed is a toy. All she was doing was

bouncing up and down on it like it was a trampoline. When she was little she used to do it on Mom and Dad's bed.

I read another book about that girl. That is six books down and four to go. I will write the report tomorrow.

AUGUST 7—WEDNESDAY

This is really about last night.

I was sleeping very nicely when I felt something hairy on my face and a hand grabbing my arm. I screamed like a maniac. When I opened my eyes Mindy was standing by my bed with Horsie, her teddy bear, on top of my face. "Want to sleep here," she said.

Before I could say anything Mom and Grandma came into my room.

"Want to sleep in Mikey's bed," Mindy told them, and she climbed into bed with me.

"Oh, no you don't, young lady," said Mom. She picked Mindy up and carried her, kicking and screaming, back to her own bed. She tucked her in really tight.

Mom told Mindy she had to stay in her very own new and beautiful bed, and we all went back to sleep.

It was quiet for about five minutes, then Mindy started to yell, "Horsie! Want my Horsie!" I heard Mom go in and talk to Mindy and then Mom was in my room again. Mindy's teddy bear was lost someplace. When we put the lights on Mom found it at the foot of my bed. She took it to Mindy.

This time it was quiet for about ten minutes and I was just about asleep when I heard Mindy calling out, "Water! Want a drink of water!" She kept it up and wouldn't quit and I was about to get out of bed and get her water when I heard Mom doing it.

By this time I couldn't get back to sleep. So I could hear Mindy very clearly about ten minutes later when she started talking to herself out loud: "Want my crib! Don't want my new bed. Want my crib."

She kept talking like this, loud enough to hear but not yelling. I finally got out of bed and went into her room. "Oooh, Mikey," she said when she saw me, "wanna play?"

"No playing," I said, "it's the middle of the night. Now go to sleep like a good girl."

"Want my crib," she said. "Don't want this bed."

"It's a beautiful new bed for big girls," I said.

"It stinky," Mindy said. This is her word for all things she hates.

"It's beautiful and new and very nice," I said.

"Bring back Mindy's crib," she said.

Just then Grandma came in. "What's going on?" she asked.

"Mindy wants her crib back," I said.

"Oh, dear," Grandma said. She sat down on the edge of Mindy's bed and began to talk to her. "You are too big and grown-up to sleep in a crib anymore," she said. "Now you have this beautiful new big-girl's bed. Isn't that good, Mindy? Aren't you proud of it?"

"It stinky," Mindy said.

Mom came in just about then. "What is happening here?" she asked.

"Mindy wants her crib back," I told her.

Mom groaned. "We will never sleep tonight," she said. She sat down on the other side of Mindy's bed. "Mindy is too big to sleep in a baby crib now," Mom told her. "Mindy is my big girl now and she sleeps in a brand-new and beautiful big-girl's bed."

"Want my crib!" Mindy yelled this time.

"The crib is gone," Mom said pretty loud. "No more crib!"

Mindy began to cry.

Just then Dad came in. "What in the world's going on?" he asked.

"Mindy wants her crib back," I said.

"Then let her have it back," he said, "so we can all get some sleep."

"Oh, no," Mom and Grandma said almost together.

"If we give in to her, we're lost," Mom said.

"If I don't sleep, *I'm* lost," Dad said.

By this time Mindy had stopped crying and was watching what was going on. I guess she never had a crowd like this in her bedroom in the middle of the night before.

What happened was that Mom stayed with Mindy and slept in Mindy's bed with her. The rest of us went back to our own beds and to sleep.

We all keep telling Mindy what a big girl she is. But she won't really be one until she *believes* it.

AUGUST 8—THURSDAY

Mom and Grandma were arguing this morning. "Helene made those boys wild," Grandma was saying, "they weren't born that way."

"Twins are hard to raise," Mom said.

"Nonsense," said Grandma.

"I'm sure Helene does her best with them."

"Helene is a potato head," said Grandma. "That's why those boys are wild."

That's the way it went on, Mom saying one thing and Grandma another, all the time going around and around in circles. I went away and read another one of my library books about that girl and her friends.

I noticed something that made me feel good. I was getting used to reading. I read that whole book by dinner, which is very fast for me.

I think if a book is good and you like it, you read faster.

AUGUST 9—FRIDAY

In the morning Jimmy Rossillo called me, which is amazing. We have been in the same class for two years now, but I wouldn't exactly call Jimmy a friend of mine.

I asked him how his summer was so far and he said lonely, boring, disgusting, but otherwise okay. He asked to come over, or for me to go to his house.

I went to Jimmy's after lunch. His sister was there. She is older than him. We rode our bikes to the park near his house and cycled around the running track. When we got tired we rested on a bench under some trees.

"My father hates me," Jimmy said. "He was supposed to send money for me to fly out to San Diego to be with him this month, but he didn't."

"Maybe he doesn't have the money," I said.

"He has it all right," said Jimmy.

Jimmy's mom and dad have been divorced for two years. Jimmy always seems to be either mad or sad about something. I think it is his parents.

"I never get to see him," Jimmy said.

"Well," I said, "my dad is home and I never get to see him. He's always working."

"That's different. At least he's in your house. He's around.

"And I had a fight with Mom," Jimmy said. "She wouldn't buy me a ticket to see Dad. I know she has the money. She is too cheap to spend it."

I didn't answer, mostly because I couldn't think of anything to say. So we just sat for a while.

"How is your summer going?" Jimmy asked.

"Okay," I said. "I have to read ten books. And write reports."

"Oh, yeah," said Jimmy with a grin. "The famous *Baseball Life of Johnny Bench.* Why'd you do that, anyway?"

"Stupidity."

Jimmy laughed. "I think somebody snitched on you," he said. "That's how Miss Boring caught on. And I think I know who snitched."

"Steve Mayer," I said.

"You got it," said Jimmy.

"I wish I was positively sure of it. I mean, I don't know for certain that he did it so I don't know what to do."

"I know what I'd do," said Jimmy. "Zap him."

AUGUST 12—MONDAY

Grandma will be staying only one more week. We had this little talk yesterday about my book-report problem. She laughed when I told her about handing in the same report twice. "Kids have a natural amount of foolishness in them," she said. "You can't get too excited about it." And then she said something I have been thinking about.

"You learn more from failure than success," she said.

Is that true? I think maybe it is. I thought I was the greatest actor in the class. I was so sure I would get to play Young Tom Medicine. And I didn't. So this is what I learned: Keep your thoughts to yourself and your big mouth shut. Bragging only makes you look like a fool.

AUGUST 13—TUESDAY

Brian came over and we shot some baskets, then Jimmy Rossillo showed up on his bike. So Jimmy and me played a game against Brian, who is a lot bigger than both of us. We thought we won the game, 30 to 26, only Brian said, "I thought we were playing *fifty* wins." So we did that and he beat us.

After that we just sat around. Mom brought out a big pitcher of iced tea and served it to us. When she went back in the house, Brian began giggling. "Woo, woo," he said.

"What's so funny?" I said.

"Your mom's pregnant, isn't she?" Brian said. Then he and Jimmy began laughing.

"Sure she is," I said, "so what?"

That seemed to make Brian and Jimmy laugh more. I was getting mad. And I was embarrassed. "Quit it," I told them, "just cut it out."

"Your dad's been a busy little bee," Brian said. I hated the smirk on his face. I wanted to punch it off.

"Go home, Brian!" I yelled at him. "Just get out of here, okay?"

He took his time about it, making a few more remarks, but he left.

"And you can go too," I said to Jimmy.

"What'd I do?"

"You laughed."

"I was laughing at how red your face was getting," Jimmy said.

"I don't think it's funny," I said.

"Don't have a heart attack about it," said Jimmy. "Your mom *is* going to have a baby, you know."

"So?" I barked at him.

"So be cool," he said.

"That's easy for you to say. She's not your mom."

"I've been through a lot worse," Jimmy said. "My dad took up with another woman ten years younger than him. And he and my mom fought about it every day for a year before they split. I got so mad at my dad I could hardly talk to him. I think I still hate him a little."

"That's rough," I said.

"And I haven't seen him since Christmas. I miss him every day."

It was one of the saddest things I'd ever heard. Jimmy looked like he could cry in a second. But he didn't. We hung out some more and then he went home.

Why do parents do that to kids? You would think that if they bring kids into the world they would stay together until the kids grow up. But sometimes they don't.

I don't know what I'd do if Mom and Dad got divorced. In fact, I don't even want to think about it.

AUGUST 14—WEDNESDAY

This was a day I was all alone but not lonely.

Mom needed to shop for new clothes at the mall. So she took Grandma and Mindy, but I decided to stay home and just read books.

I read *two* whole books in one day!

I can hardly believe it. It was okay. In fact, it was not even like schoolwork at all.

In fact, I really liked it!

AUGUST 15—THURSDAY

In the morning I wrote one of my reports. The book was funny so I made my report funny. Writing is getting easier and easier for me. And maybe reading is too.

I sure hope so.

I have only one more book to read and two more reports!

AUGUST 16—FRIDAY

I got up early this morning and wrote the other book report. Then Mom took me to Dr. Hertz. He checked my night brace and said I was doing fine. I knew that, anyway, because I have been good about wearing it all the hours I should.

But I still hate it!

AUGUST 17—SATURDAY

Dad went to his office later in the day, so he was home for breakfast with all of us. He said that things were a little slow in the office right now, so maybe we could even sneak in a short vacation after Grandma goes home to Toledo!

Carrie is home and called this afternoon and wanted to come over. I told her we were busy and going away from the house, which was a lie. I hope she is not going to become a pest.

I went to the library in the afternoon. When I told Stacy I needed only one more book to complete my summer assignment, she smiled. "That doesn't mean you should take out only one book," she said.

"I wasn't going to," I said, which perhaps was not the truth.

"I put aside some books for you," said Stacy. She had them under the desk in a drawer. There was a slip of paper on them with my name on it. "I think you'll enjoy these," she said.

I sat down at a table for a while and looked them over. Two were about baseball. One was a science-fiction book that Stacy said a lot of kids liked. I asked Stacy if she had a book about a kid whose parents got divorced. She went away and came back with a book like that.

So I checked out four books and went home. And I read the book about divorce, which was real sad and only a little funny. I felt really sorry about the girl in the book.

Tomorrow I will write my last report for Miss Boring!

AUGUST 18—SUNDAY

It was a crazy kind of day today, mostly because Grandma is leaving tomorrow. Dad stayed home the whole day, which is always a good day as far as I am concerned.

We went to Aunt Helene's house in the afternoon. Grandma is leaving early tomorrow, so it was her last chance to be with Helene. She also spent time with Robert and Rupert. They are very well behaved when she is around to watch them.

Before I went to bed and before I wrote this in my diary, I finished the last book report for Miss DeBoer. Yay! Yippee! Wahoo! Hooray! and zipideedoodah!

Tonight I can sleep with a clear conscience.

AUGUST 19—MONDAY

Things were very rushed and crazy this morning because Grandma had a nine o'clock plane to catch back to Toledo. So we all got up early, dressed, and rushed down to breakfast. Except for Mindy, who is always slow. Mom called me in to help get Mindy dressed because she had to run downstairs and cook breakfast. I helped put her T-shirt on and her socks, then laced her sneakers. She has the teeny-tiniest little sneakers. They are not even as big as my hand!

Grandma and Mom were so funny when we started putting Grandma's stuff in the car. Grandma couldn't find her plane ticket and got all excited. She and Mom looked everywhere, only to find the ticket was in the outside pocket of Grandma's tote bag, which was already in the trunk of the car.

Finally we set off for the airport. Grandma checked in and we walked with her to the gate. It was all so rushed that I didn't have time to get sad at Grandma's leaving. "I'll be back before you know it," she said when she kissed me good-bye.

"And when is that?" I asked her.

"In December," she said, "before the baby comes."

Mindy started crying when Grandma disappeared down the walkway to the airplane. "Want Grandma!" she yelled. Other people were staring at us and Mom scooped up Mindy and we got out of there in a hurry.

It was very quiet in the house for the rest of the day. Mom was busy organizing our clothes for our vacation, and Mindy took a very long nap. If Grandma was still here, I would have hung out with her, like we had been doing. She wasn't even gone one whole day and I missed her already.

AUGUST 20—TUESDAY

I have spent a lot of this day just thinking. I thought about two things, mostly. The new baby and Steve Mayer.

Did Steve snitch on me or not? I wish I knew. He was such a big deal the day I got caught by Miss DeBoer. And he did know I was in trouble before even I knew it. How could he know that unless he told on me? And what do I do to him if he did?

If he snitched on me he will be my worst enemy.

The baby.

I asked Mom if she wants it to be a boy or a girl and she said she doesn't care. "I will love either one," she said to me.

"I know that," I said, "but which one would be better?"

She wouldn't say. I told her I want it to be a boy. No question in my mind about that.

"Then maybe you will get your wish," she said.

I hope so.

I asked her about names. She said she hadn't given it much thought, but it would probably begin with M, like Michael and Mindy. This is after Mom's father, Myron, who was my grandfather but died before I was born.

Myron? I don't think that name is too good.

I will start thinking about boys' names beginning with *M*.

AUGUST 28—WEDNESDAY

Well, diary, you must be pretty mad at me. Because I am mad at me for forgetting to take you on our vacation.

It was a pretty good vacation. Having Dad all to ourselves for a whole week was wonderful. And Mindy behaved pretty good as well.

We started out driving toward Boston. We stopped in some nice motels that had swimming pools. In New York State we saw Cooperstown and the Baseball Hall of Fame. That was a great day. We spent about three hours there. I saw so many exciting things. Babe Ruth's big bat, Ty Cobb's glove and spikes, and lots of films about players and some World Series. I wanted to go back again the next day, but we drove on to Massachusetts.

We stayed in an old inn in Stockbridge, Mass. In the olden days, people would go there by coach and horses. We picnicked by a lake the next day. Mom brought bread and milk and stuff and made sandwiches. It was a great day.

Then we went to Boston. We stayed in a big motel outside of town that had a pool and was on a river. Dad and me took out on one of those boats that you pedal with your feet. It was nice, and when I got tired Dad did most of the pedaling.

I saw Bunker Hill and where the Boston Tea Party was held. Then we drove to Lexington and Concord before heading back to our motel.

Boston is a really big city. Dad got us lost a few times and we drove around a lot. Mom was reading the map but she couldn't find out where we were. We kept passing Fenway Park and turning back around. So I said we should stop and get tickets for a ball game the next time we pass it. And Dad did that!

We saw the Red Sox beat Cleveland, 6 to 3. A really good game.

In the Faneuil Hall Market I bought a bunch of postcards. I sent one to Libby, even though I know she is away. Also to Jimmy Rossillo at home and to Dolf at Camp Sha-Kah-Nah-Kee.

We took only two days getting home.

I was a little sad when we got here. The vacation was over and school starts next week. I opened all the windows in my room and let in the air. Then I sat down on my bed and thought awhile.

What I thought was this: A vacation is not like real life. But I always want it to be. We had one week of driving around together, eating all our meals together, spending twenty-four hours a day with each other. It made me feel like I want to be with Mom and Dad—even Mindy—more than I do.

Now I am back to real life. Mom will cook, clean house, shop, and do the laundry like she always does. Dad will go back to work, leaving home every day and hardly being around. We will not have as much fun and be together in the same way until next year.

And that makes me feel a little sad.

AUGUST 29—THURSDAY

I had some postcards waiting for me when we got home last night. Libby wrote from Maine, where her family always rents a house for August. She said she was having a good time riding horses, learning to play tennis, and swimming every day.

Dolf sent me a letter from camp. He says he misses Ned.

Ned wrote me from Camp Lean-Too. He hates it there. He says he misses Dolf and also misses real food.

YAAAAAHHHHH!

I just realized something. Next week I will be back in school!

The summer is almost over.

AUGUST 30—FRIDAY

I hated today.

Mom got my school clothes organized and made me try on all my winter shirts and pants. My flannel shirts are too small, and also most of my corduroy jeans.

In the afternoon we went to the mall. I tried on about 100 pairs of new pants. Mom and Mindy came into the dressing room with me and there was hardly room for the three of us. Also, it was hot in there. I put pants on and took them off. Mom kept putting her hand inside my waist and tugging to see if I had room in there. I kept putting my sneakers on and taking them off. Mindy kept getting in the way. Then she had to go to the bathroom. Mom took her and they were away for the longest time. I sat there in my underpants, trying not to die of the heat. When Mom came back she brought flannel shirts with her. And two sweaters. I said if I put on a shirt and a sweater I would probably melt. Mom said, "Do it." I did it.

I was very glad to get out of that dressing room alive.

Then we bought a new winter jacket. By this time Mindy started acting up. Mom said she was cranky because she was missing her nap. I told her I was cranky too. She laughed at that. When we got home Mom turned on the air conditioner in her bedroom and we all hung out up there, sucking in the cold air. Mindy and Mom fell asleep on her bed, and I fell asleep on the floor.

AUGUST 31—SATURDAY

It set a record for heat today, 96 degrees.

Mom and Mindy and me decided we would go to the beach to cool off. So Mom started making all these sandwiches. I wanted bologna and Mindy wanted peanut butter. Mom made some of both and also tuna fish. Then she filled a thermos of cold milk for Mindy and put some juice in the picnic jug. I found our old beach chair in the garage and brought it out to the car.

All this took a long time. I was really impatient to get started for the beach. I was thinking about jumping into the water and being really cool.

Then Mom remembered that she wanted the beach umbrella, because Mindy has delicate skin and can't take too much sun. I went back into the garage and found it. By this time it was nearly noon.

As we began to leave Mom reminded me to take the garbage out, so I picked up the bag of garbage, the picnic jug, and the bag of sandwiches on the way out to the car. I dropped the garbage into the trash can, put the rest of the stuff in the car, and we were off at last.

The beach was very crowded and it was a long walk from where we parked the car. But I didn't care because I could feel the cool breeze from the water.

We found a spot near the water. I took off my shirt and sneakers and ran like a bullet into the water.

After a while I got hungry. So I went back to our spot, toweled myself dry, and waited for Mom to pour me some juice and hand me a sandwich. When Mom opened the sandwich bag we got a surprise.

All there was in the bag was garbage!

"Michael," said Mom, "the sandwiches—"

"Oh, no!" I said.

"You dropped the sandwich bag in the garbage—"

"And I put the garbage bag in the car."

We looked at each other for a second, then both of us started laughing at once. "What?" Mindy asked, but Mom and me were laughing too much to answer. It was one of the stupidest things I had ever done in my life, but it was funny too.

"What do we do about lunch?" I asked Mom when we'd recovered from being hysterical.

"Well," Mom said, "you could have some perfectly lovely coffee grounds and orange peels."

I started laughing again.

In the end we walked across the hot sand and had hamburgers and sodas at the outdoor stand behind the beach. And when we told the story to Dad at dinner Mom and me laughed like crazy all over again.

SEPTEMBER 1—SUNDAY

I remembered to say "rabbit" last night and this morning, so maybe my luck will get better.

This is something Carrie told me, but I haven't tried it until now. It happens when a month changes. You say "rabbit" the last thing at night, then the first thing in the morning on the first day of the new month. And you are supposed to have good luck all month.

I don't know if I really believe it, but it can't hurt to try.

It was a really good day today. Dad stayed home and

cut the grass, with me helping. I like to work with Dad
when he asks me to. I swept the driveway and helped
Dad unload the grass clippings. I love the smell of cut
grass. It smells like summer.

I told Dad about what Mom said about naming the
baby. He smiled and then said if it was okay with Mom
it was okay with him. I told him Martin is a name I like.
Then the baby could be Marty, for short. I asked him if
he had any ideas.

"Mischa," he said.

"What?"

"Maximillian is good too," he said. "Or Murgatroyd."

His face was so serious I couldn't tell if he was kidding
or not. Then, as I looked at him, he busted out laughing.
"You really want it to be a boy, don't you?" he asked me.

"Sure do."

"Well," Dad said, "you've got a 50-50 chance. But
girls are nice too."

"I'll bet you a dollar it's a boy."

"Okay," said Dad. "But if it's a girl, please don't be
disappointed. Sisters are good and sweet, and they'll
look up to you, Mike, because you'll be their big
brother."

So that was my bet with Dad. It will be worth much
more than a dollar if the new baby is a boy.

Except if they call him Murgatroyd.

SEPTEMBER 2—MONDAY—LABOR DAY

Dad was home again, two days in a row! In the afternoon we had a cookout. Laura Drager, her husband,
Fred, and her two little girls came over and Dad cooked
chicken on the barbecue grill.

It was a sunny day, but not too hot. Libby telephoned

to say she and her family were home from Maine. She said she had a great summer. I told her about my book reports, all finished and done and ready to hand in.

After the company went home I stayed outside in the backyard with Dad. The end of summer, I was thinking. That's what Labor Day is every year, even though fall begins later in September. And no matter how long the summer looks in June, it is always too short at Labor Day.

Dad moved close and put his arm around my shoulders. "Are you getting ready for school?" he asked. "Book reports all done?"

"Yes."

"I want you to start thinking about school a little more," he said. "You're a smart kid, Mike, but you don't always show it."

You're right, I thought, but I didn't say it. I have never spent one single extra minute on my schoolwork. I do what I have to, and that's it.

"I want you to go to college someday," he said. "I don't want you to scramble and struggle like I did. I got out of high school and I thought I knew everything, Mike. Which shows you how dumb I was."

"You're not dumb," I said. "You're the smartest and the best father I know."

Dad gave me a little hug. "Just do your best, Mike," he said. "But make sure it is your best."

"I'll try," I said.

We stood together for a few more minutes, but we didn't say anything more.

SEPTEMBER 3—TUESDAY

The last day of freedom before school.

Libby biked over and we hung around in the afternoon. She looked so suntanned and healthy, different somehow. When I mentioned this to her, she smiled. "I had a haircut," she said, and only then did I really see what was different. No more braid, or pigtail, or whatever you call it. Now Libby's hair was shorter, only down a little below her neck. She looked great.

We had a slight argument when she wanted to go to the library. She had to talk me into it. "You don't just read because you have an assignment, birdbrain," she said. "You read because it's fun. Because it keeps your brain alive." She gave me that look of hers that says you are a complete idiot. "Get your library card and let's go."

So we went.

SEPTEMBER 4—WEDNESDAY

Here are the good things about school:

1) You see your friends again after the summer
2) You can play sports with enough people on each team
3) I can't think of a third good thing

Here are the bad things about school:

1) Everything else

The best part of the first day of school was that it was only half a day. Libby, Ned, Dolf, Jimmy Rossillo, and Carrie are all in my class.

We got out of school about noon, in time to go home

and have lunch. But first we all milled around in the
school yard. Ned Robbins told me about his camp, and
Dolf did the same. We all agreed to go shopping for
school supplies with Libby tomorrow.

Mindy was carrying on when I got home. Mom told
her that I had gone to school and she said she wanted to
go to school too. When Mom explained that she is too
little, she screamed her head off.

Poor little dumb kid. When she is my age she will
know better.

SEPTEMBER 5—THURSDAY

We went to regular classes today. I have Mr. Pangalos
for homeroom and social studies. Kids say he is tough
and that you can't kid around in his class. We all sat
down next to our friends, like we always do, but Mr.
Pangalos made us sit according to alphabetical order.

At the end of the period we went to language arts and
it was Miss DeBoer again. We just talked about what we
did over the summer and had a good time. At the end of
the period she asked me to stay, and then she said I
should come and see her at the end of school.

The day kind of dragged. After the summer, being
cooped up in school for a whole day seems like a lot.

I sat down in the chair by Miss DeBoer's desk. She
looked over the book reports I gave her and she was a
little surprised at some of the books I had read. "You
seem to be widening your horizons," she said, which I
didn't really understand. Then she talked about a contest a magazine was sponsoring. It was a poster contest
to get more kids to read books. "You may be an expert
in that subject now," she said with a smile. Anyway,

now I am supposed to think up an idea for a poster. And hand it in to Miss DeBoer by the end of the month.

It's really unfair. I did my assignment over the summer. Why should I have to do an extra assignment now?

I met the gang later and we went to Dealtown. Lots of other kids from school were there. I bought a loose-leaf book with NFL team logos on it. Then I bought paper, section dividers, and index cards. And I bought a whole ten-pack of ballpoint pens. Mindy sometimes takes my pens and doesn't bring them back. As I walked around the corner of the aisle I almost bumped into Steve Mayer. "Well, look who's here," he said. Billy Alston was standing alongside Steve. "Did you have a good summer?" Steve said, smiling at me.

There was something in his smile and his voice that ticked me off. He seemed like a real wise guy, which he is anyway. "Terrific," I said to him, "no thanks to you."

Steve grinned at me again. "Tell me," he said in a nasty way, "did you finally learn how to read?"

"Close your mouth before I put a sock in it," I said.

"Ten whole books," Steve said, "how did you ever manage it?"

That did it.

I dropped my shopping basket on the floor and took a hard swing at Steve's grinning face. But Steve ducked and I ended up smacking Billy Alston, who yelled real loud and socked me in the face. So I grabbed him around the waist and we wrestled each other to the ground, yelling at each other.

Mr. Atkins came running from the front of the store. "No fighting in here," he said. He had a tight grip on my arm and on Billy's. Meanwhile, Steve Mayer was standing off to the side, looking like it was a big joke, shaking his head from side to side. I wanted to go after him again, but by this time Libby and Ned were between us.

Steve Mayer and Billy went up to the front of the store, bought their supplies, and left. I picked up my stuff from the floor and stood there, really steamed. "I'll kill that Steve Mayer," I said. "I'll take his eyeglasses off and stomp them into the ground."

"And you'll get yourself in trouble again," said Libby.

"I don't care," I said. "He snitched on me and I've got to get him back for that."

"You don't really *know* he snitched on you," Ned said.

"Of course he did," I said. "He had to be the one."

"I don't think so," said Libby. "Steve Mayer is a show-off, and obnoxious, but he's not a snitcher."

"Then how did he know I was caught before even I did?" I said.

Libby shrugged.

There really was no answer to that question, the same one I'd been thinking about since June. How else could Miss DeBoer know what book report I'd handed in the term before? She wasn't even in our school that term. Somebody must have told her, and that someone had to be Steve Mayer.

"Your eye looks funny," Ned said, "kind of puffy and red."

When he said that I felt it. Billy Alston must have socked me there, but I was too excited to even notice it before. Now it was beginning to hurt a little.

We gathered our school supplies, paid for them, and left. Libby walked me partway home. I didn't say much, but I was thinking a lot. Now I had one more person to put on my list of people I'd hit: Billy Alston. And he hadn't done anything.

Mom noticed my eye right away. I told her what happened and she was angry. "Fighting is not the way," she told me. "Two days of school and you're in trouble again. Your dad will speak to you tonight."

I was thankful for one thing: I didn't have any homework.

SEPTEMBER 7—SATURDAY

I have a real black eye now.

It doesn't hurt but it sure looks funny. I talked to Dad last night, but it was so late I'm writing what we said today.

I knew what he was going to say before he said it.

Fighting is wrong.

(Right, Dad.)

You should never start a fight.

(Of course, Dad.)

Punching someone never solves anything.

(Right again, Dad. But how about if it makes you feel better? I didn't say that, of course.)

People who snitch on other people will get their own punishment by not having any friends.

(Except for Steve Mayer.)

In the end Dad said he would not punish me for fighting. My black eye, he said, that was punishment enough.

So I at least had one thing to be happy for.

SEPTEMBER 8—SUNDAY

My eye has a purple ring around it, with some red near my nose.

Dad worked today, but we managed to have break-

fast together. He took a long look at my eye and asked me if it hurt. I told him only my feelings were hurt.

It turned out to be a quiet day. I picked up one of the books Libby made me take out of the library and began to read it. It was not the kind of book I usually like at all. It was science fiction. A small boy in it has this rare blood disease. His sister, Meg, is terrific. She reminded me of Libby.

What was amazing is that I liked the book. I read about half of it very quickly, and I think I will write my first book report on it.

After dinner Mom stopped washing the dishes and had a surprised look on her face. "Oooh," she said, and she put a hand on her stomach.

"What is it?" I asked her.

"Your little brother just said hello," she said, smiling. Then she took my hand and put it on her stomach. "Wait for it," she said. In a few seconds I felt it! A little kind of kicking against my palm.

"That's the baby," said Mom.

"Hello, Murgatroyd," I said.

SEPTEMBER 10—TUESDAY

Every kid in school today was staring at my eye, talking about my fight with Steve Mayer and Billy Alston, asking me about it or making funny remarks to me.

"Did your little sister punch you out?"

"What happened to the other guy?"

"Looks like you had a fight with yourself and lost."

I tried to pay no attention.

I sat with Libby, Dolf, and Ned at lunch. Even they kept staring. Today my eye was purple and red, but getting yellow around the outside.

I may end up with the first rainbow-colored eye in history.

SEPTEMBER 11—WEDNESDAY

Tonight I stayed up late to finish the book. Wow, was it terrific.

I am amazed that I read that whole book in just a couple of days. And now I have to read the book that was written before this one. Libby says it's great.

I think I will try to read a book a week. That's really not too hard to do. And if I read a book a week, that would be fifty-two in a year.

In ten years I would read over five hundred books!

Five hundred BOOKS? If I did that, my brain would probably have so much stuff in it I'd have to drag it around on wheels!

SEPTEMBER 12—THURSDAY

After school I got my bike and went to the library. And the book I was looking for was in! I grabbed it off the shelf fast so no other kid could get it.

Mindy has a new habit. She will watch any game show on TV. But now she is talking along with them.

When I walked past the living room after dinner she was watching *Wheel of Fortune.* And I heard her talking along with the announcer.

"A brand-new Ninety-Eight Olsmobile," I heard her say.

A little later I heard her say, "A get-away vacation in France."

Maybe she will be an actress on TV when she grows up.

SEPTEMBER 13—FRIDAY

T.G.I.F. Even though it is Friday the thirteenth.

The first whole week of school is a drag. I think we should start slowly. The first week we should go only one day. The next week, two days. And so on.

That way we would get used to it better. We could gradually get used to getting up so early, spending six hours in school, and doing homework when we get home.

This is a terrific idea, and if I knew who was in charge of school, I would write him a letter about it.

SEPTEMBER 14—SATURDAY

I got an invitation in the mail to Libby's birthday party. It had a telephone number to reply, so I called up at once. I spoke to Libby's mother and said, "Yes, I will come to the party."

Libby's mom asked my name. When I told her she said, "Oh, yes. Michael Marder. How is your eye doing?"

I think the whole world knows about my eye by now.

SEPTEMBER 15—SUNDAY

Dad had to work for just a little while, so he took me with him to the office.

On the way there Dad asked me how school was going. I told him about Miss DeBoer and the extra reading-poster assignment she gave me. "I think it's unfair," I said. "It's like a punishment."

Dad looked at me. "Michael," he said, "remember we talked about doing your very best? And trying a little harder?"

"Miss DeBoer hates me."

"I don't think so," Dad said. "It sounds more as if she likes you. She must think you're good enough to do this poster. So you could say she has confidence in you."

Why did the assignment sound better when my dad said it than when Miss Boring did?

SEPTEMBER 16—MONDAY

Well, it happened again.

Every year I dread going back to school in the fall. I imagine that the school will burn down, or some other thing will happen, and then the summer vacation will go on and on and on.

And then school begins. And it is never as awful as I think it will be.

That happened today. I just got up and went to school and I *knew* all my summer dreams were gone. This was real life. My life until next June, anyway.

It was even an okay kind of day.

I understood everything in math. Social studies class was interesting, even if Mr. Pangalos wasn't. Miss Boring wasn't. For gym we had a class softball game in the school yard. Mom made me my favorite sandwich, leftover roast beef with a little catsup. And nobody had anything to say about my eye, which is only a little purple, maroon, and yellow now.

I'm back in school. It's okay, I guess.

I can stand it for another year.

SEPTEMBER 17—TUESDAY

Maybe my dad is right. That's what I have been thinking.

I know, deep in my heart, that I have never really

given school my full and complete attention. I have not done one thing extra.

Only what I had to do.

But from now on I am going to change my ways. Because I just figured something out. School is my job.

Just like my dad has work, and Mom works in the house, my job is in school. So I might as well do it as well as I can.

It's a little scary, but I won't die of studying.

So tonight I started to think about that reading poster for Miss DeBoer. I lay back on my bed and stared at the ceiling. The ceiling is just a white square with a light in the middle and a few cracks here and there. The cracks look a little like a railroad track in the snow.

While I was tracing the railroad route across the ceiling, I thought of an idea.

Read a book a week.

That's what I was thinking for myself a while ago.

And if every kid did that, we would have a country full of smart people. So maybe that is the slogan for the poster.

READ A BOOK A WEEK

I will think some more about this.

SEPTEMBER 19—THURSDAY

Libby was really weird today.

We walked home from school together and stood talking for a long time. Then we sat down on someone's lawn and talked some more. Libby's birthday party is a week from Saturday.

"What kind of games will we play?" I asked her.

Libby shrugged. "The usual stupid games," she said.

"Right," I said.

Libby didn't say anything for a long time. Then, when she spoke, I could see she was nervous. "I want to ask you something, Michael, and I want you to tell me the truth. Even if it hurts."

"Okay," I said.

She looked me in the eye. "Do you think I'm pretty?" she asked. I was really surprised to hear Libby ask that, but it was easy to answer. "You sure are," I said.

"You're not just saying that?"

"Heck, no," I said. "Next to Joyce Appleman, and maybe Linda Talbott, you're the prettiest girl in the class."

Libby kind of nodded slowly. "What about my nose?" she asked.

"What about it?" I said. "It's a nice nose."

"It's kinda long, though, right?"

"No," I said. "Your nose fits your face. It's an okay nose."

"How about these eyebrows?" she said. "Don't you think they're too thick and bushy?"

I gave her eyebrows a good look. "Nope," I said. "In fact, I like them."

Libby stared into the street at a car that was passing by. She looked really sad.

"What's the matter?" I asked.

"This will be my last kid's birthday party, Michael. Do you realize that next year I will be a teenager?"

"So what?" I shrugged.

"I'm not ready for that," she said.

I started to laugh. Libby looked at me with an angry face and it only made me laugh some more. "What's so funny, birdbrain?" she asked.

"You are," I said. "You are Libby Klein. As long as I've

known you, you have always done what you want and when you want. So why will you be any different in a year or so?"

"It scares me," she said. "I don't want to be like Marcy Lipton or Carrie. Always looking in the mirror or making gooney faces at some boy."

"You won't be that way," I said.

"I will never wear eye shadow," she said.

"And I will never wear a dress," I said, which made Libby smile.

"Promise you'll always be my friend," she said.

"Always," was all I said.

"And don't ever tell anyone about this conversation," she added.

So, dear diary, I am only going to tell you.

SEPTEMBER 20—FRIDAY

I wrote my slogan on a piece of paper and showed it to Miss DeBoer. She looked at it for a second. "Pretty good," she said, but the way she said it told me she didn't think it was good at all.

"It's not finished yet," I said. "But how about the idea? Is that okay?"

"Do you think kids can read a book a week?" she asked me.

"Of course," I said.

"Even slow readers?"

"If they read more, they would stop being slow readers," I said.

"Okay," she said. Then she looked through her desk and got out the contest folder with all the rules on it. It was from a magazine called *Squink,* which I had never heard of. "Take the folder home, Michael," she said. "Maybe it will spur some new ideas."

After school I read the whole folder. Last year the winning poster said "Get Ready for Reading." It didn't look so great.

I got out a yellow pad and wrote on it.

> READ A
> BOOK A
> WEEK!

That looked plain and ordinary. So I thought a bit and then I got an idea. I wrote.

> READA
> BOOKA
> WEEK!

I liked that. It was kind of tricky. But it needed something more. So I wrote this:

> WILLYA
> READA
> BOOKA
> WEEK?

Then I stared at that awhile. And I thought that some wise guy would see that question hanging there and he'd say "NO WAY, JOSÉ."

I would like it more if someone asked me to *try* to do something.

So I wrote this:

TRYTA
READA
BOOKA
WEEK!

I stared at it for about half an hour. I liked it. I took it downstairs to show Mom. She was on the couch, fast asleep. Mindy was beside her.

I went and called Jimmy Rossillo on the telephone. He was in a funny mood because he answered the telephone in a French accent. "Ah, Mistair Marder," he said, "zees iz Jeemy."

"I know that," I said. "Look, I need your help."

"Wiz what, my fren?"

I started to tell him about the poster, but he already knew something about it. "Zee postair for Mademoiselle Boring, yes? You need zee great artiste, eh?"

"Of course, of course," I said in my own French accent, which was bad.

"Zen come right ovair," Jimmy said, "tooty sweety."

I left a note for Mom on the kitchen table and biked over to Jimmy's house. He was still in his French mood when I got there. "Excellentay," he said when he looked at my slogan.

"You really like it?"

"Oui, oui," he said. "It will be mahvellous."

I gave him the folder Miss DeBoer gave me. "I see eet in red, white, and bleu," Jimmy said, "like zee French flag."

"And when will you have it?" I asked.

"Tooty sweety," he said, "like Monday."

I grinned at him and he grinned back. "San Diego for Christmas," he said, "think about it."

"You're going to see your dad?"

"Exactement." He grinned at me. "He already bought the supersaver airplane ticket and sent it to me. Santa Claus in a red bathing suit. Building snowmen on the beach."

"A palm tree for a Christmas tree," I said.

"You got zee idea," he said.

I left the stuff with Jimmy. He just would not quit being a phony Frenchman. And I know he will do a good job on the poster because he is a good artist.

Or *artiste*.

SEPTEMBER 22—SUNDAY—
FIRST DAY OF AUTUMN

I got this paperback book of baby names off my mom's night table and looked through it. And I discovered something: A lot of the *M* names are weird.

Who would name a kid Malcolm? Or Malachi? How about Manfred?

Give a kid a name like that and they will probably grow up to be very strange.

Madison is not a bad name, but it is more a last name than a first. Manuel, Marshall, and Marlow are not too good either.

I guess I am lucky to get a name like Michael. It could have been Mason, Maxwell, Maurice, or Mercer.

Or Murgatroyd.

SEPTEMBER 23—MONDAY

I waited for Jimmy outside of school. When he came along he told me he did not have the poster. "Why not?"

Jimmy shrugged. "I did it a couple of different ways and I couldn't decide which one I liked best."

We agreed to work together after school. I really was anxious to get the poster finished and give it to Miss DeBoer.

Jimmy's house was kind of sloppy. The breakfast dishes were still on the table. Upstairs, Jimmy's bed was mussed up and his pj's were in a ball on his pillow.

I looked at three different versions of the poster Jimmy had made. Two of them had books on them with the number "52" on the cover of the books. I didn't get it.

"A book a week is fifty-two books a year," he said.

Of course. I felt like a dummy. But then I thought, if I don't get that idea, maybe nobody else will, either. I told Jimmy I hated the 52. He said he liked it. We argued for a long time.

Finally, we decided to start over. In the end we had a nice poster, with the slogan written on a book. It really looked good. Jimmy said he would do it over more neatly and bring it in tomorrow.

I walked home. When I got to my house Mindy was in the front yard. The minute she saw me she ran into the house yelling, "Mikey's home! Mikey's home!"

Mom was waiting in the kitchen, and she was really angry. "Do you know what time it is, young man?" she asked.

I looked at the kitchen clock over the sink: 6:15. Oh, oh. Now I knew why Mom was so mad.

"I have called Libby Klein's house, Nathaniel's house, and the school. Nobody knows where you went. Not one soul, Michael. I was about to call the police."

Mom came walking across the kitchen and I thought

she was going to whack me. But instead she grabbed me in a big hug and started crying. "I was so worried and scared," she sobbed.

After a minute or so she sat me down at the kitchen table, blew her nose in a tissue, and I got the lecture. About all the kids who disappear, who go off with strangers and get killed.

I knew all that. I had been hearing it ever since I started going to school alone. It always scared me, but I knew it was true. There are a million maniacs out there who like to hurt and kill kids. There are a million kidnappers who offer kids rides and candy and then take them away and never bring them home.

I felt like a stupid jerk. All I did was go to Jimmy's house, but I never told Mom.

Diary, you belong to a fool.

SEPTEMBER 25—WEDNESDAY—YOM KIPPUR
This is really about yesterday. Jimmy brought the poster with him to school and we gave it to Miss De-Boer after class. She put it up on the file cabinet near the wall and walked away for a minute, then turned around and stared at it. Jimmy and me were waiting for her to say something. When she smiled we both felt relieved.

"Excellent," she said. "Very creative."

Jimmy smiled at me and I did the same to him.

"Thanks to both of you," she said, "I think this poster has a real chance to win a prize in *Squink*'s contest."

"What would we win?" Jimmy asked.

"Let's cross that bridge when we get to it," said Miss DeBoer. "But win or lose, you've both done yourselves proud."

Jimmy said, "So long," and took off. I hung around while Miss DeBoer gathered things from her desk and put them into folders. "Could I talk to you for a minute?" I asked her. "I've been wondering about something. About last term."

Miss DeBoer looked at me. "Yes?"

"About that stupid thing I did," I said. I couldn't even get myself to say "book report."

Miss DeBoer said it for me. "That's past and forgotten, Michael. I'm sure you won't cheat on a book report again."

"No," I said, "but how did you know? Mrs. Gruen moved away and then you took over last term. So how did you know I handed in the same book report twice?"

Miss DeBoer opened a bottom desk drawer and took out a blue folder. "Mrs. Gruen left this for me, Michael. It's an evaluation form for all the kids in the class. And in it was the title and grade she gave you on your last book report."

Well, it wasn't Steve Mayer after all. And I was a fool again.

"Would you like to hear what Mrs. Gruen said about you?" Miss DeBoer asked.

"Michael Marder," Miss DeBoer read from the sheet in her hand. "An excellent writer. Real flair and imagination. Reading level below par. Must be motivated to do more. Spelling, top in class. He has potential to do much better work." She put the sheet back in the folder. "Does that sound like you, Michael?"

"Yes," I said. "Last term. I think I am motivated now. And I know I improved in reading."

"I think so too," said Miss DeBoer.

That made me feel good, but that other thing in my mind almost crossed it out.

All the time I was wrong. I blamed Steve Mayer for snitching on me and he never did.

What should I do now?

SEPTEMBER 27—FRIDAY

Tomorrow is Libby's birthday party so after school I planned to go shopping for her present. I had about $25 in the secret desk drawer in my room. But I didn't know what to get for her.

"A handkerchief is always nice," my mom said.

"A handkerchief?" I said. "Who wants a handkerchief?"

"Something lacy and frilly," Mom said. "Girls like that kind of thing."

I almost laughed out loud. "Libby's not like that," I said.

"Stationery is always appreciated," Mom said.

"I'd hate it if someone gave me stationery," I said.

"Nice writing paper and envelopes?" Mom said. "I think it's rather sweet."

"I was thinking of something personal," I said. "Libby is one of my best friends."

"You mean, perhaps something she could wear?"

"Yes," I said. "But I don't know what."

"You don't know her size, do you?" asked Mom.

"Yes," I said, "she's an inch shorter than me."

"That doesn't tell me anything," Mom said. She thought for a minute. "A scarf," she said, "buy her a nice scarf."

"You mean something woolly to wear when it gets cold?"

Mom laughed. "No," she said. "I mean something bright and colorful to wear around her neck."

That was a good thought, but a scary one. I would have to go into a woman's store and ask some lady to help me pick out something I did not know the first thing about. "Mom," I said.

"Yes," Mom said, smiling at me. "I'll buy it tomorrow. How much do you want to spend?"

"Less than twenty-five dollars," I said. "A lot less."

"Okay," Mom said. "Leave it to me."

Every boy should have a mother as nice as mine.

SEPTEMBER 28—SATURDAY

I didn't even get to see my present for Libby because Mom brought it home all gift-wrapped. It cost $8.00.

The party wasn't until seven o'clock so I spent the day reading this book about a boy whose parents get divorced. It made me think of Jimmy Rossillo a lot, although the dad in the story stayed in the same town.

I started to get dressed about five when Mom came in and made a big fuss about me taking a shower. I hate it when she does that. I am as clean as I have to be, I think. When I get all sweaty, like after playing ball, I always take a shower. I change my underwear every day, and I shampoo my hair when it needs it.

Dad came home after I got dressed. "You look pretty sharp, sport," he said to me. "Heavy date tonight?"

"Only a party," I said.

"With members of the opposite sex, I assume."

"It's Libby Klein's birthday party," I said.

"They will swoon when they see your big brown eyes," Dad said.

"What's swoon?"

"They will faint dead away."

"Dad," I said, "come on." He always embarrasses me when he talks that way. Like I was so handsome girls will chase me down the street. Who would want girls to chase them down the street, anyway?

Mrs. Klein answered the doorbell when I rang. "Michael," she said, "hello. You look smashing."

"Hello," I said. I always feel shy when I go to someone's house alone, and parties make me nervous too.

There were a bunch of presents on a table near the wall, so I put mine among them. Libby was wearing a shiny white dress. She looked terrific. "Happy birthday," I said to her.

"Thanks," she said, "but it's not really until Tuesday."

"You look great," I said.

Libby made a face at me. "My knobby knees are showing," she said.

Before I could say anything some other kids came in and Libby walked away to say hello. But I was kind of amazed that someone as great as Libby could be worried about how she looked.

I went into the dining room to get a soda. As I turned around with it in my hand, Steve Mayer was standing there. We just stared at each other for a second. "You better not hit me," Steve said.

"I wasn't going to hit you," I said. "In fact, I owe you an apology."

"Keep your apology," Steve said.

"Okay," I said, "then I take it back."

"Just stay away from me," he said, and started backing away.

"Listen to me a second," I said. "I thought you

snitched on me about my book report. Then I found out you didn't."

"Why would I snitch on you?" Steve said. "You can get into trouble all by yourself."

"Well," I said, "I thought you did and I was wrong."

"I don't care what you think," Steve said. "You're not my friend."

"You don't *have* any friends," I said.

"Certainly not a nerd like you," Steve said.

NERD! I really wanted to belt Steve right then, but I didn't. I was so mad I couldn't get any words out. Steve just gave me that smile I hate and walked away back into the living room.

We stayed away from each other for the rest of Libby's party. And Steve Mayer is right: I am not his friend and I will NEVER NEVER be his friend.

SEPTEMBER 29—SUNDAY

Before Dad went away to his office he said Mom was not feeling well and that I should be extra nice today. "Try to be helpful, Mike," he said, "and keep Mindy out of Mom's hair."

So I cleaned up the kitchen and then took Mindy upstairs. She wanted to play StratoMatic Baseball, like she has seen me do with my friends. I explained to her that you have to know something about baseball to play it, and also you have to know how to read.

"I can read," she said.

"No, you can't," I said. I didn't say it too strongly because I didn't want to get her mad. Mindy jumped up and got this little book. It's called *Baby Boo* and Mom has been reading it to Mindy forever. She opened to the first page and began to read it. "I am Baby Boo," she said, just like she was reading. "I am a baby just like you. I have a mommy and a daddy just like you."

"Wait a minute," I said. "Mindy, you're not reading— you've just memorized that book."

Well, that was a whole concept she didn't understand and I had to explain it to her. "I can read!" she insisted. She grabbed my hand and practically dragged me down to the kitchen, went into the pantry, and started pointing at boxes. "Cheerios, Sugar Smacks, Maypo," she called out. Then she went to the refrigerator and pointed to the little sign on it. "General Lectric" she called it.

It was kind of amazing for a little kid, but it still wasn't reading. I gave her a hug and told her she was terrific. "And Mindy can read," she said.

"Yes," I said, "Mindy can read."

Sometimes you have to lie a little to keep the house quiet.

SEPTEMBER 30—MONDAY

We started a whole new project today in social studies: ancient Egypt. People back then were very strange.

They made these huge tombs and put themselves inside in a boat. They also did lots of pretty disgusting things. Like storing their brains in jars. Of course they were dead at the time.

Mr. Pangalos let us pick our own report groups, so I got Libby and Jimmy Rossillo.

OCTOBER 1—TUESDAY

I forgot about saying "rabbit" this morning and getting good luck for a whole month. I remembered last night, though. But this morning, when I went downstairs to breakfast, it just slipped my mind. So I won't have good luck this month, but maybe I'll have *half* good luck.

OCTOBER 2—WEDNESDAY

When I got home from school Mom was sitting at the kitchen table with a bunch of tissues in her hand and she looked like she had been crying. I asked her if anything was wrong, but she shook her head. "Just the Wednesday blues," she said, "pay no attention."

"Can I do anything?" I asked.

"Nope," she said, sighing. "I am just fat as a house and it's a long way until January."

"Until Murgatroyd is born, you mean," I said.

Mom grinned at me. "We will not call him that," she said. "Murgatroyd, indeed." Then she smiled.

"I like Murgatroyd," I said, just to kid around. "We could call him Murgy for short."

"No way, José," Mom said.

"But Martin is better," I said. "Then we could call him Marty for short."

"I like Mitch for a nickname," Mom said. "And Shelly for Michelle."

"Marty is better than Mitch."

"Well," said Mom, "anything is better than Murgy."

OCTOBER 3—THURSDAY

We had our Egypt report committee meeting after school. We started out meeting in the living room, but Mindy came in to watch this kid's program on TV, so we went up to my room. That's where we had the argument.

I wanted us to do a report on the battles of King

Thutmose III, who conquered a lot of land for Egypt. Jimmy thought that was a bad idea, mostly because he had his own. He wanted to write about tombs and tomb robbers. Libby wanted us to report on the flooding of the Nile.

By the time we each had our say and fought around about it, it was time for Libby and Jimmy to go home. As he was leaving Jimmy gave me this little picture of a mummy that he had made into an advertisement. Under the picture it said, "When You Go West, Go With the Best—Ankhamon Undertakers." I thought it was funny but Libby didn't.

I think it's going to take a couple of *weeks* before we can even decide what our report will be about.

OCTOBER 4—FRIDAY

Jimmy is really a funny guy.

Today at lunch he handed me a comic strip he had been drawing in Miss DeBoer's class. It was entitled "SuperThut!" And in the strip he made Thutmose into a kind of Superman character, flying around in the air.

We got ten minutes for a committee meeting in class. Libby still was stuck on agriculture. I told her I thought that growing wheat was just about the most boring thing I could think of. How armies fought with spears and shields was a lot easier to write about and more exciting. Jimmy didn't seem to care anymore. He just doodled and shrugged when I asked him which was better.

So we agreed to meet at Libby's house next week.

OCTOBER 5—SATURDAY

Mom and Dad went to a wedding tonight. But the bad part is that Mom got Doreen to be our baby-sitter again.

I had a big argument with Mom about it. I am almost eleven and a half years old. I can watch Mindy and stay by myself.

"It's all arranged," Mom said.

"Then unarrange it," I said.

"We're going to be out very late, Michael."

"So what?" I said. "I can go to sleep by myself."

"Michael, puh-lease!" Mom snapped at me. When she uses that kind of voice I know the argument is lost. So I turned around on my heel and stalked away to show her how mad I was.

Mom was all upset and nervous before she and Dad left. "I should have bought a new dress," she told Dad.

"You look fine," Dad said. "Like a lovely pregnant woman."

"I just didn't want to spend the money," Mom said.

"Honey, you're beautiful," Dad said.

"I should have spent the money," Mom said. "I look like a cow."

As soon as Mom and Dad drove away Doreen went into Mom's room and began using her perfume and her eye shadow. "You are a sneak and a perfume robber," I said to Doreen, but she just ignored me. "Go watch TV," she said.

I went downstairs and did just that. I hate Doreen. She always talks to me as if I was five years old.

When I went into the kitchen for a drink of water, I could hear Doreen's voice from Mom's room above.

She was on the telephone. I picked up the wall phone in the kitchen and listened. "Come on, Marty," she was saying, "you know I miss you."

"How much?" this guy named Marty said.

"You can find out by coming over, sugarpuss," Doreen said. And then she made some disgusting kissing sounds into the telephone.

"Okay," Marty said, "I'll be by in a while."

"No you won't!" I said into the phone.

"Get off the phone, Michael!" Doreen yelled, so I hung up the phone and went back to the living room. In a couple of minutes she came downstairs. "That was a nasty thing to do," she said.

"If he comes over, I'll tell my parents," I said.

"I hate watching brats like you and your sister," Doreen said.

The doorbell rang about half an hour later and Doreen came into the living room with this tall guy. He had brown hair and a lot of zits all over his face.

"Time for bed," Doreen said. "Run along, Michael."

"It's not even ten o'clock," I said. "I'm staying right here." And then I made believe I was still watching this picture on TV.

Doreen and Marty went into the kitchen. I heard them open the fridge and the clink of bottles. I waited until the commercial was on and went into the kitchen.

Doreen was sitting on Marty's lap and they were kissing. They also had glasses of beer in front of them on the table. "Hey!" I said. "That's my dad's beer. You shouldn't be drinking that."

Marty groaned and stopped kissing Doreen. "What is this kid, a spy?" Marty said.

"He's a rotten brat," Doreen said. "Get out of here, Michael!"

"Don't let me bother you," I said. "I'll just watch."

I thought Doreen was going to jump off Marty's lap and begin chasing me, but the doorbell rang, so Doreen went to answer it instead. At the door there was a guy in a T-shirt that said "Sal's Pizza" on it and he had a pizza in his hands. "Doreen, baby!" he said to her, "I didn't know this was your pizza."

"Hello, Sid," Doreen said. She took money out of her jeans and paid Sid.

"How 'bout I come back later?" Sid said. Then he looked past me and saw Marty in the living room. "Oh," he said, "you already got company. Marty Pizzaface."

"Get out of here, Sid!" Marty yelled at him.

"You gonna make me?" Sid growled. Before I could even think about that Sid came charging into the house. Marty ran past me to grab him and Doreen started screaming "No! no!" and got between the two guys and that's when the pizza box got knocked up in the air and the pizza fell out of it and landed facedown on the carpet.

Doreen stopped yelling and Marty and Sid stopped wrestling and they all just stared at this upside-down pizza on the blue carpet.

"I gotta go," Sid said, and he left.

Marty got down on his hands and knees and began picking up the pizza slices and putting them back into the box. But a lot of the cheese and sauce was still sticking on the carpet. Marty looked disgusted. "I thought you stopped seeing Sid," he said.

"I have," Doreen said. She was scraping up cheese

from the carpet. A lot of it was still sticking, though, and the sauce was all over.

"The carpet is ruined," I said.

"And you're going to tell your parents," Doreen said.

"Well," I said, "I think they'll see it for themselves."

Doreen got some cleaning stuff from under the sink in the kitchen and she and Marty worked on the carpet for about an hour. "Mrs. Marder will have my head for this," Doreen said.

"If you hadn't jumped between us with the pizza, it wouldn't have happened," Marty said.

"That's right," Doreen said, "blame it on me."

Well, they started arguing and wouldn't quit. And the stain didn't look like it was ever going to come out. After a while I went to bed.

I don't think Doreen will be our baby-sitter again. And I decided I don't like the name Marty anymore.

OCTOBER 7—MONDAY

I woke up to go to school this morning and felt funny. Mom sat me down in a living-room chair and stuck a thermometer in my mouth. I had a 101° temperature. "No school for you," Mom said.

I got back into my pj's and into bed. Mom brought up a big pitcher of orange juice and told me to drink as much as I could.

After lunch my temperature went up to 102°.

I felt awful. Everything in my body hurt. Mom gave me aspirins and I fell asleep.

OCTOBER 8—TUESDAY

Mom took my temperature but would not tell me what it was. She called Dr. Gilner. He is coming over later.

I tried reading this school book, but my eyes hurt. Mom says I must have some kind of flu. I started coughing and my nose is stuffed.

Dr. Gilner has a nice happy way about him, always smiling and joking. "You look like a sick puppy," he said when he came into my room. He looked down my throat, listened to my lungs, felt my pulse, and looked in my ears with his light. "Well, Michael," he said to me, "it looks like you have what all the other kids have. In about a week, you'll feel better." Then he wrote out a couple of prescriptions for my mom to have filled and went off to talk to her.

I fell asleep.

OCTOBER 9—WEDNESDAY

Mindy and Mom were standing in my doorway when I woke up today. It was after nine o'clock. "How is my Mikey?" Mindy asked. She has been a very good girl. Mom told her not to go near me, and so far she has stayed away.

"I think I feel a little better," I told Mindy. I didn't have a headache anymore. But when I coughed I got a sharp pain in my chest. And I still couldn't breathe.

When Mom read the thermometer I still had a temperature of 102°.

I can't write anymore.

OCTOBER 10—THURSDAY

Today my temperature dropped under 100° for the first time since Monday.

After school I called Libby and Jimmy. They are still not agreed on what we should do about our report, but Mr. Pangalos gave us more time because so many kids in class are absent.

My mom is a wonderful lady. She keeps smiling and joking around and she is just so gentle. Just her cool hand on my hot head makes me feel so good.

Sick kids would be in a lot of trouble if they didn't have mothers. And I guess there are some kids who don't. Who takes care of them? Who brings them juice and soup and makes sure they take their medicine?

It's almost too hard to think about, being sick and not having a mom.

OCTOBER 11—FRIDAY

My temperature was 98.6° this morning! And I feel a lot better, except for my cough and my nose running. I must have used a million tissues this week.

In the afternoon I got out a schoolbook on Louis Pasteur and I read a lot of it. Louis Pasteur was this French doctor who found out a lot about germs. He was a good scientist and a terrific guy.

I have been thinking about maybe becoming a doctor when I grow up. I would be able to help people when they were sick, like Dr. Gilner does. I used to think I wasn't smart enough to be somebody important like a doctor. But now I am changing my mind. I have a brain.

And if I try hard enough and study long enough, I bet I could do a lot of things.

I will think some more about this.

OCTOBER 12—SATURDAY

No temperature all day yesterday. So today I got dressed and did not spend all day in bed in my room.

The doorbell rang about four o'clock and when I answered there was Jimmy Rossillo on his bike. "Don't come too near me," I said, "I may still be catching." Jimmy came inside and sat down at the opposite end of the living room from me. He said I didn't miss a thing in school all week. We sat and talked for a little bit, but then we ran out of things to say.

"I better go," Jimmy said, but he still sat there. "Listen," he said, "I got a question to ask you. Are you still Carrie's boyfriend?"

"I never was her boyfriend. And I am definitely not her boyfriend now."

"Okay," Jimmy said.

"Why did you want to know about Carrie?"

Jimmy shrugged. "She wants me to be her boyfriend."

I started to laugh. That was Carrie, all right. She had to have a new boyfriend every term.

"What's so funny?" Jimmy asked.

"Nothing," I said. "Do you really want to be her boyfriend?"

Jimmy shrugged. "I don't care."

"It's not too bad," I said. "She'll kiss you sometimes, she'll hang around with you a lot. If she gets too clingy, just tell her to buzz off."

"Okay," Jimmy said. "I wanted to make sure you didn't care."

"No," I said, "I don't care at all."

I watched Jimmy ride away down the street. I felt like cheering. Carrie was now off my neck for once and for all.

OCTOBER 13—SUNDAY

Mom had a big argument with Dad today. She is really starting to feel tired now. And she didn't want him to stay at the office all day. So they fought about it, and Dad went off anyway.

Grandma called from Toledo. She was all upset when I told her about my flu. "Is your nose still stuffed? Of course it is, I can hear it."

"It's not too bad now."

"Well," she said, "here's what you do. Tell your mom to make some of the camomile tea I left. And then she should make you a bomb with the lemon grass."

"What? A bomb? Grandma, what do I need a bomb for?"

She started laughing then. "Not a bomb," she said, "a balm—spelled b-a-l-m. It's a kind of lotion. You rub that balm on your upper lip and it'll clear your sinuses right up, Michael."

I started laughing then. I kept seeing this tiny bomb made out of lemon grass with a fuse burning at the end of it. I stick it up my nose, it explodes, and my sinuses are fixed forever because my head gets blown off.

I must be almost cured now because my sense of humor is coming back.

OCTOBER 14—MONDAY—COLUMBUS DAY

After dinner today I was stacking dishes in the dishwasher and Dad was washing a pot when we heard Mom calling from the living room. "Hank," she called out, "I need you."

So Dad and me ran into the living room. Mom was sitting on the couch. Our couch is big and brown and built kind of low to the ground. It's very soft and comfortable.

"I'm stuck," Mom said, "I can't get up."

We both stared at her.

"Will you help me, please?" Mom said. She stuck out her hand. Dad and me each took one of Mom's hands and pulled her to her feet.

"This belly is too much to carry around," Mom said. She looked embarrassed.

Dad started laughing. "And it's not funny!" Mom said, walking away. "It is not funny at all."

That made me think of something true, dear diary. When people say something is not funny it usually means the joke is on them.

OCTOBER 16—WEDNESDAY

Back to school again.

In Miss DeBoer's class we were reading *Tom Sawyer* and were almost halfway through it. That meant I had some catching up to do.

Last term that would have put me in a panic, but I was a much better reader now. The language in that book is a little old-timey, but the story is terrific.

After school Libby, Jimmy, and me walked back to

my house together. We had to agree on our report because Mr. Pangalos wasn't going to give us forever.

Libby was mad at me, but I didn't give in. I still think
agriculture is one of the most boring things in the
world.

Finally we agreed that we had to decide tomorrow,
at the latest. Before he left Jimmy gave me this drawing
he had been doodling. It showed two canoes racing on a
river. Jimmy made it into a kind of advertisement that
said, "Nile River Racing! Saturday, at Abu Temple
Raceway!"

After dinner I went up to my room and began reading *Tom Sawyer.* After a while I started looking at Jimmy's drawing again. It would be good if we could get his
comic strip and the ads he had drawn into our report.

Then the idea hit me.

What has comic strips and advertisements? *A newspaper!* That was it: We could make our report in the
form of a newspaper. We could have Jimmy's stuff in it,
I could write about Thutmose's battles, and Libby could
write her stupid agriculture story.

The name of it jumped into my head: *The Nile News.*
I called Jimmy on the telephone and explained it. He
got all excited for once. "Yeah," he said, "and we can do
more cartoons and we can do a classified ad section.
Like 'Space to rent in well-kept tomb.'"

"I love it," I said.

"Have you spoken to Libby yet?" Jimmy asked.

"Nope."

"Good luck," said Jimmy.

Jimmy was thinking exactly what I was. Libby is a
great person, but she does like to have her own way. If

she didn't like the idea of doing *The Nile News* we were sunk.

I thought about it a little, then remembered what I had just read in *Tom Sawyer.* The part in the beginning, when Tom acts like he doesn't want anybody else to whitewash the fence and the kids end up paying him to do the work. We had to make Libby think of the newspaper idea by *herself.*

I called Jimmy back and explained it to him. "Michael," he said, "you are definitely sneaky. But it's a great idea."

We'll do it tomorrow.

OCTOBER 17—THURSDAY

Jimmy and me got together with Libby at lunch today. Carrie was there as well; she sticks to Jimmy like glue. I brought Jimmy's comic strip and his advertisements along. "It would be good if we could use these in our report," I said. "But I don't know how comic strips and ads go with agriculture."

"Yeah," Jimmy said. "I sure wish there was a way to get it in our report."

"We should think about it," Libby said.

"Right," I said. "And I've been thinking about a recipe for smoked hippo."

"Smoked hippo?" Libby said. "That's stupid."

"No, it's not," I said.

"Wait a minute," Libby said. Jimmy and me could see her thinking. We waited.

"No," Libby said, almost to herself, "that won't work."

"What won't work?" Jimmy and me said together.

"Recipes, comic strips, ads," Libby said. "It all sounds like a newspaper—"

"A newspaper?" Jimmy said.

"Hey," I said, "a newspaper! Libby, that's it!"

"I love it!" Jimmy said.

"Do you really think so?" Libby said.

"I can see a headline now," I said. " 'Nile Floods—Wheat Planting Begins.' And you write your agriculture report like a newspaper story."

"The Nile News!" Jimmy said. "That's the name of our newspaper."

"The Nile News," Libby said. "That's good."

Well by now I really was laughing, and so was Jimmy. But Libby didn't catch on, or else she thought we were just happy at solving our report. We kept on talking about it right until the end of the lunch period. It was such a good idea even Carrie liked it.

The Nile News lives!

OCTOBER 18—FRIDAY

I spent most of the time after school writing an in-person interview with Thutmose III. Along with Libby's "Nile Floods" story, that will be the front page. Up in one corner, though, we'll have a weather report for Thebes.

Libby says she is going to write two editorials: "The Cattle Tax—Priestly Folly" and one about making a speed limit on how fast chariots should go.

We are having fun.

OCTOBER 20—SUNDAY

Mindy caught my flu and she is as sick as I was. Poor little thing, she looks so pale. I sure hope Mom doesn't get sick.

We now have three pages of *The Nile News* and we'll probably have more. We will paste it all together and use the copier in Dad's office to make the actual newspaper. It's going to be great.

We had to write a character sketch about a member of our family for Miss Boring. I decided to write about the new baby, even though it is not actually in our house yet. Here is what I wrote:

MY NEW BROTHER

My new brother's name is going to be Mitchell. We will call him Mitch for short, and he is going to be very short until he grows up. He will not say anything to me for about a year or more, but I will do a lot of talking to him. He will mostly stare at me, but after a while he will get to recognize me and he will probably smile when he sees me.

Some people say that babies are messy and boring to have around. They are very tiny and helpless and they take a lot of caring for. They cannot eat sandwiches for several years. They can't use the bathroom. They don't know the language. They really don't know how to act and behave at all, and you must be very patient.

So what is the sense of having a new baby in your house? Well, it makes the family bigger. When I grow up I will have somebody else in the world with my name who is my brother. Wherever I go or Mitch goes, we will be thinking about each other. And both of us will help Mindy. And when our parents get old we will all help them if they need us.

If Mitchell is a girl, we will call her Michelle. But I hope she is a boy.

OCTOBER 22—TUESDAY

Jimmy and me won a prize in the reading-poster contest!

Miss DeBoer made an announcement in class this morning. She got a telegram from *Squink* magazine saying that our poster was one of the winning entrants. Details would follow, it said.

Later, our principal, Mr. Guma, interrupted all classes to make an announcement about Jimmy and me on the school intercom.

During lunch a few kids came over and congratulated us. They wanted to know what prize we won, but we couldn't tell them because we don't know yet.

This was a great day.

OCTOBER 23—WEDNESDAY

Mom was still in bed this morning and Dad said she has caught Mindy's flu. He brought up some tea for Mom and I took Mindy's breakfast up to her room. She is not too good at blowing her nose and she was a mess.

By this time it was too late for me to make my lunch, so I had to make sure I had money to buy a school lunch. Dad said he would stay home until I got back from school today, so I shouldn't be late.

Jimmy and me asked Miss DeBoer to look up what the first prize is again and she did. It is a trip to Washington, D.C., next April to see the cherry blossoms. But it is a trip for only one winner and one member of his family. Jimmy and I cannot go together.

Ned, Dolf, Libby, and Jimmy saved a place for me at lunch while I went through the line.

"So what do we do?" Jimmy asked me when I sat down. "We both can't go to Washington."

"I think it's very cheap of them," Libby said. "If you both did the poster, you both should go."

"I would want my dad to go with me," said Jimmy. "That would be one extra time I could see him next year."

I had already figured out what I would do. My dad would be too busy to go with me, and Mom would have the new baby and probably she couldn't go. "I would have my grandma go with me to Washington," I said.

I could see the sad look on Jimmy's face when I said that. A part of me wanted to say, "Okay, you can have the trip, Jimmy." But another part of me was wanting that trip for myself.

"Maybe you both can go," Ned said. "Maybe Jimmy's dad can pay for himself and Michael's grandma can also pay for herself. Then the four of you could go."

"I don't think so," said Jimmy. "My dad can just about pay to send me one ticket to see him a year."

"This stinks!" Libby said. "You shouldn't have to decide who's going to go."

"But we have to," I said. "How can I invite my grandma to go with me if she has to pay for herself? That's wrong too."

"You should flip a coin for it," Dolf said. "That's the only fair way."

"I'm not going to do that," said Jimmy. "This is too important to me. I would have another whole weekend with my dad. Michael can get to see his dad every weekend and every day."

I didn't like the way everybody looked at me. I felt like they all wanted me to give the trip to Jimmy, like I was selfish for wanting it for myself. "I hate this," I said. "Let's talk about something else."

We didn't talk about anything after that. And the more quiet it was, the more I was feeling bad about it.

I had a lot on my mind when I got home, but I didn't have time to think about it because I had to take over the Sick Patrol from Dad.

He took off for the office and I went upstairs and stayed with Mindy. Dad had put the little portable TV in her room and she watched a game show until she fell asleep.

I really felt bad about what was happening between Jimmy and me, but I felt worse when Jimmy called me later. "Michael," he said, "I don't want you to take this wrong. And I still want to be your friend. But I really think you should let me get the trip to Washington."

I didn't know what to say, so I said nothing.

"It wasn't a poster until I did it," Jimmy said. "So I think I deserve the trip more than you."

"Is that so?" I said. "Well, it wouldn't have been a poster unless I had the idea first."

"You just made up a slogan. But it wasn't a slogan contest—it was a poster contest."

"And if my slogan hadn't been good, we would not have won," I said.

"So what do you say?" Jimmy went on. It was like he wasn't hearing me at all. "Will you let me have the trip?"

"No," I said, "I won't."

"Thanks a lot," Jimmy said sarcastically, then he said good-bye and hung up.

OCTOBER 25—FRIDAY

We handed in *The Nile News* to Mr. Pangalos today and it was a big hit. It was also all spoiled because of the prize-contest argument between Jimmy and me.

I had a long talk with Dad during dinner last night. I told him all about Jimmy's phone call and the bad feelings I had. He listened to everything and then he asked me, "Did you earn the right to go to Washington?"

Sure, I told him.

"Then you deserve to go on the trip," Dad said. "Now, the next question is, does Jimmy deserve to go?"

"Yes," I said.

"Then he should go too," Dad said. "Your teacher should flip a coin to see who gets the trip."

I had to ask Dad about this feeling I had about me going and leaving Jimmy behind. "If that happens," I said, "I will feel very bad about it."

Dad smiled at me. "That shows you have a good heart, Mike. But you guys will still have to flip a coin. Unless you want to just let Jimmy have the trip as a gift from you."

"Like heck I will," I said.

"Then you've answered your own question," Dad said.

So I was very clear about things when Jimmy kind of cooled out toward me in school.

At lunch he didn't talk directly to me. We sat with Libby and Carrie, Jimmy's new shadow, and if you didn't know he was mad at me you probably wouldn't even see it. But I knew it and I felt it.

On the way home we met just outside of school. "You didn't change your mind, did you?" he asked me.

"Nope," I said. "We should flip for it."

"No," he said, "I need that trip more."

"Well, you're not getting it from me," I said.

With that, Jimmy turned away. And that meant I had lost a friend.

OCTOBER 27—SUNDAY—DAYLIGHT SAVINGS TIME ENDS

We had two sickies in the house and Dad stayed home both days.

Sunday night Dad went out and brought home some Kentucky Fried Chicken. Mom was feeling good enough to come down and join us at the table. It was the first time in ages that we all had a meal together. Mom looked pale and still sick in her blue robe. "I don't have my legs under me yet," she said when she walked into the kitchen. "Sure you do, Mommy," Mindy said. "I see them."

Well, we all had a laugh at that. And it was a good dinner.

I spent the night reading the rest of *Tom Sawyer*. It was a very good book, and the part I liked best was when Tom went to his own funeral.

I wouldn't go into a cave if you paid me a million dollars.

OCTOBER 28—MONDAY

Mom felt good enough so that Dad could go off to work today. But she is still not well enough to make dinner, Dad said. I told him that I would make dinner tonight. He looked at me and laughed. "Okay," he said, "you're on. What will you make?"

"I don't have any idea," I said.

"Sounds wonderful," Dad said. "But whatever you cook, I guarantee I will eat."

So I went off to school with my mind on food.

I ate lunch with Libby, Dolf, and Ned. I asked them about cooking dinner and what was easy to do. Only Libby had some ideas. "Spaghetti," she said. "You make a big pot of boiling water, put in the spaghetti, and cook it about ten minutes. Then you pour the whole thing into a colander to drain off the water."

"What's a colander?" I asked.

"It's a printed thing with the months and days on it, stupid," Ned said.

Libby ignored that. "It's a big bowl with lots of holes in it," she said. "And when the water drains off you just get a jar of sauce and put it on the spaghetti."

I told her that sounded too hard to me, that all I ever made was French toast and scrambled eggs.

"So why don't you make that?" Libby said.

That's what I did. I used about eight eggs and lots of bread and we all had French toast. Mom and Dad said it was good. And Mindy loved it. "It terrific, Mikey," she said to me.

"It's terrific," Mom corrected her.

"It's terrific," Mindy repeated.

Mindy is talking a little bit better every day. She uses new words all the time. I'm beginning to think she gets them from her game shows.

She was talking to herself in the bathroom tonight

when I walked by. I heard her say, "A seventeen-foot runabout with outboard motors." It was really spooky.

Maybe she *is* watching too much TV.

OCTOBER 31—THURSDAY—HALLOWEEN

It was Mindy's second Halloween for trick or treating and she had a big fight with Mom. At first Mom was not going to let her go out, because of her just getting over being sick, but Mindy carried on so much that Mom had to let her. She was allowed to go, but only in the afternoon after school, and I went with her.

Mindy wanted to be a Smurf. But there was no way Mom could make that costume. So Mindy had to be satisfied with lipstick and makeup, her own long dress, and a hat of Mom's with lots of tissue paper inside. For some reason Mindy thought this outfit made her a princess.

We went off ringing doorbells. "Oh, it's Mindy Marder," said Mrs. Leahy, our next-door neighbor.

"No," said Mindy, "I'm a princess."

"Well, you're a beautiful one," said Mrs. Leahy. She dropped a Hershey's miniature in Mindy's bag. As soon as we started walking away Mindy unwrapped that little candy bar and stuck it in her mouth.

This is what Mindy collected just from our street: five wrapped sucking candies, two fun-size Mars bars, three wrapped peanut chews, two Hershey bars, six pennies, and an apple. Mom inspected all the loot before she let Mindy take it up to her room.

Our doorbell kept ringing as kids came around for their treats. Mom posted Mindy at the door to give out our candy, which was peanut chews and Milky Way miniatures. In between callers, Mindy kept eating the Milky Ways.

I hadn't spent a lot of time deciding on my costume. But I let Mom draw a fake beard on my cheeks with eyebrow pencil and she wrapped one of her bandannas around my head and I went out as a pirate.

Outside on the street I met Brian Beam and we walked around together. It was getting really dark by this time. We rang Mrs. Toffenetti's doorbell a few times, but no one answered. But when we looked through the window there was Mrs. Toffenetti sitting in a chair and watching TV. She is an old woman whose husband died five years ago. "Look at the old bat," Brian said, "she must be deaf." He rang the bell a couple of more times. "Wake up!" he yelled.

"Come on," I said. "She probably doesn't even hear us."

"Hey, man," said Brian, "this is trick-or-treat time. We don't get a treat, we got to play a trick, right?"

"No, we don't," I said. I started going down the porch steps. When I looked back Brian had a black marker pen in his hand and was making a big X right across Mrs. Toffenetti's white front door. "Hey," I yelled at him, "stop that!"

He was laughing when he came down the steps to me. "She's probably too cheap to buy candy," he said.

"You're an idiot," I told him. "She's an old lady. How's she going to get that off her door?"

"Hey, man, not my problem," he said.

I was disgusted with him. "Stay away from me, Brian," I said, and I crossed the street to get away from him. He was a stupid kid, which I knew before, and I will have nothing to do with him anymore.

I met up with Dr. Schaeffer and his two little kids, Willie and Mary. Mary was dressed all in black, like a witch, and Willie had a Superman costume on. Neither one of them had a lot of teeth when they smiled.

I walked around with the Schaeffers for about another hour. It was fun, but not as exciting as it used to be.

I think I'm getting too old for Halloween.

NOVEMBER 1—SATURDAY
Yesterday I said "rabbit" right before I went to sleep and when I woke up, so I know I am going to have good luck in the month of November. I sure hope so.

I saw Stacy at the library this afternoon and I met Libby there. We walked our bikes down the street and looked over our books. I was very lucky and found a new baseball book. And another one about this fat kid that I heard was funny.

Mom took Mindy to the supermarket with her today, and later to see the doctor Mom goes to for the baby. His name is Dr. Kliot and I have never met him.

Wait a minute, that is wrong. I met him once when I was being born. Other than that, I don't know him at all.

I called Jimmy to see if he wanted to come over tomorrow, but his mom said he wasn't home. I asked her to have Jimmy call me back. Just because he is mad at me is no reason to bust up our friendship.

But he never did call.

NOVEMBER 4—TUESDAY—ELECTION DAY
Before Dad left for work today he asked me to rake and bag the leaves on our lawn. He said he would pay

me a quarter a bag, which was nice since I was going to do it for nothing anyway.

I packed six big leaf bags full and made a dollar and a half. It took me all afternoon. I guess I will use the money for Christmas presents.

I save all year but after Christmas I am always flat busted.

NOVEMBER 7—THURSDAY

Mom and I always disagree about when I need a haircut. She says I need one now, but I think it is just about right. "It's curling down over your collar," she said.

"I like it that way," I said.

"I will have to get you a violin," she said, which must be some kind of joke because I don't understand it.

But I will get a haircut tomorrow—without fail—and that is not a joke.

NOVEMBER 8—FRIDAY

When I got to John's Barber Shop, Jimmy Rossillo was sitting in John's chair getting his hair cut. I said, "Hi, Jimmy," to him, but he didn't say anything back to me. He just made believe I wasn't there. I felt like a fool. And then I felt mad.

I picked up a magazine and pretended to read it, but I was steamed. When Jimmy left I sat down in John's chair. "Do you know Jimmy or what?" John asked me.

"I know him," I said. "We used to be friends, in fact."

"So what happened?" John asked.

I didn't want to talk about it, so I just said, "Stupidity."

John laughed. "There's always a lot of that going around," he said.

NOVEMBER 10—SUNDAY

Ned called and said I should come over after lunch for some touch football. I biked over to his house and Dolf was there. Ned's big brother, Jamie, played with us, and whoever had him on his side won. He is seventeen and very fast, as well as tall.

Later we went inside and had milk and peanut-butter cookies, made by Ned's grandma. They were terrific, but Ned didn't even have one of them. He just drank skim milk, because he is on a diet.

The diet is working. Ned is almost a normal-size person now. His willpower is amazing.

NOVEMBER 11—MONDAY—VETERAN'S DAY

It was rainy and cold and miserable all day.

I spent the day reading a lot and thinking a little. I finished another book about the girl whose baby brother is a genius. It was good.

I finally told Mom about what was going on—or *not* going on—between Jimmy and me. She agreed with me that it was dumb. "But people are that way sometimes," she said, "not only kids. Aunt Helene didn't speak to me once for about three months, and she's my sister."

"What did you fight about?"

"It's so long ago I don't remember. But it wasn't anything important."

"Well," I said, "I still want to be Jimmy's friend, but he doesn't want to be mine. And it's bugging me."

"Hang in," Mom said. "Either Jimmy will change his

mind and you'll be friends again or he won't. Friend-ships have to work two ways."

I am thinking about that now. And I guess it's true.

If I liked Carrie better, maybe I would have been a real boyfriend.

NOVEMBER 13—WEDNESDAY

We had our first prep test for the spelling bee. Miss DeBoer let us study this long list of words that may be used. Then we got a short test on the first twenty words. I got them all correct.

I am a great speller. I have always been a great speller, except for mixing up *dairy* and *diary* when I was only a little kid. I really should have won the class spelling bee last year. But who could tell that *calliope* had two *l*'s in it? Besides, I have never seen or heard a calliope in my life.

NOVEMBER 15—FRIDAY

At lunch today I sat with Libby, Ned, and Dolf. Carrie came along and sat down with us. Then Jimmy came off the lunch line, looked around for Carrie, and when he saw her sitting near me he sat down someplace else.

Everybody knows that Jimmy is not talking to me.

Some kids agree with Jimmy, and the rest with me. Ned thinks we are both crazy and should flip a coin and forget it. I have told him a million times that I am willing to do it. But Jimmy won't.

I'm sorry there was a poster contest at all because I have lost a friend.

NOVEMBER 16—SATURDAY

This week is Mindy's birthday and I wanted to buy her present today. I asked Mom about it. She said that it should be a toy of some kind or maybe a doll. But not any doll that is shown on TV. Mom says they take advantage of kids and make them crazy to buy stuff. So we never get any of those.

I remember when I was little how I wanted some toy cars that I saw advertised on all the Saturday morning TV shows. But Mom would not buy them for me. I cried and cried and carried on, but she would not give in.

I went off to talk to Mindy and I heard her before I found her. She was in my room, blowing on my wooden train whistle. "Hey," I said, "quit it. That's my whistle. Just put it down."

She blew it in my face, of course. I sat down on my bed and gave her a hard look. It didn't do any good. "Mindy," I said, "it's going to be your birthday. What kind of toy do you want?"

"Strawberry Shortcake Doll, but Mom won't let," she said.

"Right," I said. "What else?"

She shrugged. "A two-wheeler bike."

That made me laugh. Mindy really wants a bike, but it is way out of my price range. "What else?"

She shrugged again. "Something to play with," she said, "chocolate, and nothing to wear."

I went off to Dealtown to see what to buy for Mindy. Mr. Atkins saw me come into the store and he said, "Hello, it's the prizefighter again. What was that about, anyway? You punching that kid?"

"It was a mistake," I said.

"I'm glad you didn't hit him on purpose," said Mr. Atkins.

I walked away to the toy department and looked around for about fifteen minutes. There were some things to buy Mindy but they cost too much. And there were some lower-priced toys, but they were from TV.

And then I saw that there was an Etch-A-Sketch on the shelf. It made me mad to see it again because I used to have one. I loved playing with it, watching the little lines move around and make a design. And I would still have it if Mindy hadn't dropped it on the tile floor in the bathroom and broken it.

It cost just about what I wanted to spend. It would be fun to buy it for Mindy, because then I could borrow it from her to play with. So I took it off the shelf and walked to the front where Mr. Atkins was.

As he was wrapping it up I saw this little music box on the counter. It had a picture of Mickey and Minnie Mouse on it. When I turned the little crank it played:

> "You are my sunshine,
> My only sunshine.
> You make me happy
> When skies are gray.
> You'll never know, dear,
> How much I love you.
> Please don't take
> My sunshine
> Away. . . ."

It made such a tiny and happy sound I had to smile. "How much is this?" I asked Mr. Atkins.

"Two dollars."

"Okay," I said. "I'll take this."

"Instead of the Etch-A-Sketch?"

"No. I'll take them both."

After all, I have only one sister.

NOVEMBER 17—SUNDAY

Dad and me worked outside today. It was a great fall day, clear and sparkling and not cold at all. We raked leaves and by now we almost have them all.

Afterward, when we put the garden tools away in the garage, I saw Mindy's new two-wheeler bike. It was hidden in the corner of the garage, behind the stack of lawn chairs.

"You got Mindy's bike," I said. "Isn't she kind of young for a two-wheeler? I didn't get a bike until I was six."

"Well," said Dad, "she's a holy terror on her trike. And she has been asking for a two-wheeler." He got the bike out from the corner. It was a metallic purple color with little gold stars on the fenders, and it had training wheels on it. It was a really cute little bike.

"Can I ride it?" I asked.

"C'mon, Mike," said Dad. "You have your own bike. Besides, your feet would drag on the ground."

He was right, of course. But I still wanted to ride that little bike.

Sometimes I realize that in many ways I am still a little kid.

NOVEMBER 18—MONDAY

Well, neither Jimmy Rossillo nor me won the great *Squink* magazine reading-poster contest.

Or we both won.

But neither one of us is going to Washington, D.C.

Because we won third prize. We both get subscriptions to *Squink* magazine.

Miss DeBoer called us both up to see her after class today and told us. She said we should be very proud, that over two hundred posters were submitted to the contest and winning third prize was a fine achievement.

"It's okay with me," I said right away, but I could see that Jimmy was disappointed. He had a sad look on his face.

"It was a stupid contest," said Jimmy.

Miss DeBoer looked surprised when Jimmy said that. "No, it isn't," she said. "Getting more kids to read is very important, Jimmy. And you both represented the school very well."

"Well," said Jimmy, "the prizes stink. I'm going to throw the stupid magazine away when it comes." And with that Jimmy turned around and marched off out of the room.

"What got into him?" Miss DeBoer said.

"He was hoping to see his dad," I said. And then I explained it to Miss DeBoer.

She shook her head. "I'm sorry Jimmy feels that way," she said, "but I'm still glad you won. Jimmy will get over it."

I went off in search of Jimmy, but I didn't find him. After school I waited outside. Then Carrie showed up and I knew Jimmy would be along.

He still looked depressed when he came out of the school door. He saw me waiting with Carrie and he scowled, but he didn't say anything. I began walking with them.

"Jimmy," I said when we got to the corner where I

turn off, "is there anything I can say to be friends with you again?"

Jimmy thought for a minute. "You don't have three hundred dollars for a supersaver ticket to San Diego, do you?" he asked.

"Not at the moment," I said.

"Well, what good are you?" he said.

"Not much," I said.

"You got that right."

"You're still going to San Diego for Christmas, aren't you?"

Jimmy nodded. "But then I won't see him again until the summer. And only if he sends another ticket. Which he didn't do this year."

"Jimmy," I said, "that's not *my* fault, is it?"

Jimmy thought about that and grinned. "It should be, but it isn't." He started to laugh. "Ah, monsieur, zee logic, eet is not my best subject."

"Exactement," I said in my terrible accent.

"See you later, ma fren," Jimmy said. I stood and watched them walk away and I felt really good.

Jimmy makes me laugh, and vice versa. And that is a good friend to have.

NOVEMBER 20—WEDNESDAY

It's Mindy's birthday. My little cute sister is four years old today.

I suppose I am her idol. Sometimes I guess that she thinks I was put in our house to be her playmate and friend. And maybe I was.

Anyway, when Mindy came down to breakfast today, Mom and me both said "Happy Birthday" to the birthday girl. And Mom made her French toast, which is her favorite breakfast.

I'm supposed to scoot home from school today to help Mom with Mindy's party. But before I left for school I got the music box out of the drawer I was hiding it in and gave it to Mindy at the breakfast table. She unwrapped it and looked very disappointed until she twirled the crank and the music came out. Then she giggled. It makes me laugh too. "You are my sunshine," I said to her as I went off.

After school I just cut out for home and got there in record time. When I opened the door I was amazed. Robert and Rupert were chasing each other through the living room and into the dining room. Laura Drager's two kids were screaming on the floor. A couple of little boys from down the street were yelling at each other and throwing blocks. And Mom was sitting in a chair with her head back and a wet cloth on her forehead.

Just then Aunt Helene came running by. "Help me catch the boys," she yelled. I took off in the opposite direction from her and grabbed Robert—or maybe it was Rupert—as he shot out of the kitchen. A second later the other twin came running by and I grabbed him too. I held them for Aunt Helene.

In the middle of all this the stereo was playing much too loud and three girls plus Mindy were dancing in the dining room. Aunt Helene took Robert and Rupert from me. "This party is over," she declared, and marched out the front door with the boys.

Laura Drager was at the sink in the kitchen washing chocolate cake off the dress of a small round girl who was crying her eyes out. "Michael," she said, "am I glad to see you."

"What happened?" I asked her.

"It just went on too long."

I went to Mom, who opened one eye and looked at me. "Would you turn off the stereo, please?" she said.

When I turned the stereo off Mindy started yelling. "Hey, calm down," I told her, "Mom has a headache."

"We wanna dance!" Mindy yelled at me.

"Put your coats on and dance on the lawn," I said. "No more dancing in here."

I guess I said the right thing, because Mindy and the three girls ran out the front door—without coats—followed by the girl from the kitchen with the chocolate-stained dress.

Then the doorbell rang and it was our neighbor from down the street, come to collect her two boys. I was glad to get their coats and see them leave. Outside on the lawn, Mindy and the four girls were jumping into a leaf pile.

Laura went outside and collected her two girls. And then another mother came and took the remaining girls away. Mom didn't even move from her chair the whole time. I guess she was sleeping.

I got Mindy upstairs and washed her face and hands, which were filthy. Then I got her shoes and socks off and put her in her bed. She was out like a light in two seconds.

It's a good thing Mindy has only one birthday party a year.

NOVEMBER 21—THURSDAY

Mom and Dad had a big fight tonight right after supper. It began when Dad went off to work on some papers and forgot to clean up the pots. Mostly Mom was saying "You've got to help me more" and Dad was coming back with "I've got to earn a living for all of us."

It's the first time in a long while they had a fight. And it makes me dippy. I watched TV with Mindy, but I had one ear on what Mom and Dad were shouting in the kitchen.

I hope this was their last fight.

NOVEMBER 22—FRIDAY

We started a new routine today. Dad got up and gave me and Mindy our breakfast while Mom slept late. So he made my lunch for me while I was having my cereal.

Mom seemed in a happier mood when I got home. She sat and listened while I told her about school.

A little later we were talking about the baby. It will definitely be named Michelle if it's a girl. But Mom came up with a new name if it's a boy. "Mace," she said. "It's a beautiful and distinctive name."

"Mace?" I said. "I hate it. Mitchell is much better."

"Mace Marder," Mom said with a dreamy look on her face. "Fantastic."

"I hate it."

"It's not *your* name, honey," Mom said.

I was really mad. I couldn't believe that Mom would give my brother such a stupid name. "Mace," I said, "and what will we call him for short?"

"Gee, I never thought of that," Mom said. "Macey, I suppose."

"Macey!" I almost yelled. "It sounds *like a department store!*"

Mom looked at me and I looked at her and then we both smiled. Then we giggled. Then we laughed out loud.

So we are back to Mitchell again.

NOVEMBER 23—SATURDAY

It rained real hard all day long.

Jimmy Rossillo called in the afternoon and asked if he could come over. About three o'clock he showed up, dripping wet. We played with my electric football game for a while. Then Jimmy said he wanted to talk about Carrie.

"How do I get rid of her?" Jimmy asked me.

I almost laughed in his face, remembering that getting rid of Carrie was not easy. "You've got to work at it," I said.

"She is so boring," Jimmy said.

"I know."

"She's okay, though. But sometimes I get the idea that she just wants someone to hang out with. And if it wasn't me, it would be some other guy. How do I get her off my neck?"

"You've got to tell her you don't want to be her boyfriend anymore."

"It's like she doesn't hear me. I'm getting sick of it, Michael."

"Just keep telling her," I said. "Sooner or later she'll pick out somebody else."

We talked about Carrie for a while. She is a funny kind of girl. A boy is only a thing with her; having a boyfriend matters more.

The next girlfriend I have will be one I picked out for myself. That's for sure.

NOVEMBER 24—SUNDAY

One of the most boring days of all time.

It rained all day long, just like yesterday. Dad stayed home all day. In the afternoon he took a nap.

Mindy took a long nap. Mom did the same.

After a while I fell asleep on my bed while I was reading.

I'm too bored to write any more.

NOVEMBER 25—MONDAY

The school spelling bee begins next week, so Miss DeBoer began a practice one today. When it was my turn I spelled *u-n-f-o-r-t-u-n-a-t-e*. Fortunately, I got it right.

By the end of the class there were five of us left. Tomorrow we will have another practice spelling bee.

When I got home Mom was about to go off to the supermarket. She had a tremendous shopping list for Thanksgiving.

Mom asked me to take care of Mindy while she shopped. It was a pretty nice day out so I got her new bike out of the garage. She fit on it pretty good, except the seat was a little high for her. And the pedals are low. Anyway, with the training wheels on she began pedaling it along the sidewalk with me running alongside. I had to show her how to use the hand brakes to stop, but she got the idea of making turns right away. "You get your bike," she told me after she began to get the hang of it. So we went back to the house and I got my own bike out and we rode around the block together.

I think when she grows into the bike a bit she'll be really good at it.

NOVEMBER 26—TUESDAY

We had the play-off of yesterday's spelling bee and I lost to Libby in the final. If I wasn't so dumb, and if it wasn't so tricky, I would have won.

I spelled *d-i-s-i-n-h-e-r-i-t-e-d* right after two kids missed it. Libby spelled *r-e-s-o-l-u-t-i-o-n,* which is an easy one that is just like *revolution.* Then the words got harder. Ned Robbins missed *recognizance.* I would have missed it, too, but luckily I didn't have to spell it.

Then I got this word, *recoup.* It sounded to me like there was a chicken coop and it had to be redone. So I spelled it like it sounded to me—*recoop.*

Wrong.

Now I will never forget *r-e-c-o-u-p.*

NOVEMBER 27—WEDNESDAY

Last day before Thanksgiving and a real short school week, which is okay by me.

Mom was working like a demon when I got home. And Dad came home from work early to help.

After dinner Dad and me polished the silver and ran the good glasses through the dishwasher. Tomorrow morning we will set the table and get the house ready.

Jimmy Rossillo called. He sounded very depressed. He says that he goes to his Aunt Edna's house every Thanksgiving and it is terrible. "She can't even cook a turkey," he said. "One year when Uncle Lou cut into it, blood ran out all over."

But mostly Jimmy was thinking of his dad, who wouldn't be with him again.

A little later I went into the kitchen. Mom and Dad were at the kitchen table having a cup of tea. I don't know why, but I felt a really good feeling of love for them right then. I gave Dad a big hug, then I kissed and hugged Mom.

"Well, well," she said, "what is that about?"

"I love you both," I said. "You are the best parents."

"True," Dad said, grinning at me. He ran a hand through my hair. "And you are not a bad kid, yourself."

"We all have a lot to be thankful for this year," Mom said. "And next year, God willing, we'll have one more Marder at the table with us."

"Michael, Mindy, and little Murgatroyd," Dad said to tease me.

"Or Michelle," Mom said.

"But not Mace," I said, and Mom grinned.

So I am very happy tonight, dear diary. And I do have a lot to be thankful for.

NOVEMBER 28—THURSDAY— THANKSGIVING DAY

Busy, busy, busy.

We always have fourteen for Thanksgiving dinner every year. And we all have jobs to do. I helped Dad put two more leaves in the dining-room table, then we put a tablecloth on it and set out plates, glasses, and silverware.

Dad took Mindy and went off to get flowers while I filled our wooden nut bowls and put them in the living room. Then, one by one, I carried up our extra chairs from the basement.

Dad came back with the flowers and put them into

vases. When Mom saw them she said they needed a woman's touch and she redid all of them.

Meanwhile the house was beginning to smell great from the turkey in the oven.

Grandma called from Toledo to wish us all a happy Thanksgiving. "And I'll be seeing you real soon," she said.

A little later the guests started arriving. Cousin Joe and Emma came first, with their three grown-up kids. The only time we get to see them is on Thanksgiving. They live about fifty miles away. Then Aunt Helene showed up with Robert and Rupert. Finally Uncle Charlie and Aunt Madeline arrived.

Dad sat at one end of the table and Mom at the other. It was a great meal. It always is. I don't know why we don't have turkey, sweet potatoes, stuffing, and cranberry sauce once a week.

"Another great Thanksgiving dinner," Cousin Joe said after no one could eat or drink anything else. All the ladies started to clear and I went with the men into the living room. Uncle Charlie put the football game on TV. I sat on the floor, next to Dad, and I watched the fire in the fireplace as much as the game.

By seven o'clock all the guests were gone. Mom announced that she was exhausted. She went upstairs to take a hot shower and go to bed. Mindy was tired, too, and Dad put her to bed. Then he came downstairs and sat with me in the living room. We didn't say much as we watched the fire get smaller and die down, but it was nice just to be together.

I thought about our family. Dad and Uncle Charlie were brothers, but they didn't seem to be close at all. We hardly see Charlie and Aunt Madeline. And Cousin

Joe and Emma aren't really our cousins, I think, and the only time Mom speaks to them is to invite them to come over for Thanksgiving.

I hope I will never be that way with Mindy and Mitchell. Mom and Aunt Helene speak all the time on the telephone, and they are close, although Mom thinks Helene is a nut.

Someday I will ask Dad about why he and Charlie don't get along.

DECEMBER 1—SUNDAY

I missed saying "rabbit" last night. This is only one of the most important months to be lucky in the whole year. Christmas is coming, of course, but I was too stupid to say "rabbit."

DECEMBER 2—MONDAY

We had the class spelling bee today and I won!

Although I am probably the best speller in the class, this is the first time I ever won. I think it was because all my words were easy.

Ned Robbins and Libby went out on really hard words. After a while it was down to Rachel Beattie and me.

I spelled *macaroon* right and Rachel got *lyricist.* Then I spelled *arthritis,* which I almost missed. Then Miss DeBoer read the next word on the list for Rachel. It was *realtor.* Now that is a word that I could never miss because my dad is a realtor.

Rachel missed it. She spelled it *r-e-a-l-t-*E-*r.*

Now it was my turn and, of course, I spelled it right. Then I had to spell one more word to be the winner. No problem. It was *h-a-z-a-r-d-o-u-s.*

So now I am the champion of my sixth-grade class. Later this week I will be competing against the two other sixth-grade winners and the fifth-grade kids too. The winner will be the champion of the whole school.

How about that, dear diary!

DECEMBER 3—TUESDAY

Dad is funny about my lunch. I have only a few sandwiches that I like. Tuna fish with lots of mayonnaise in it, bologna with just a touch of mustard, or peanut butter and grape jelly.

So while I was eating my French toast, Dad asked me, "How about a leftover spaghetti sandwich, Mike?"

I gave him a funny look, but he didn't smile. He wasn't kidding. "No thanks," I said.

"I used to eat spaghetti sandwiches all the time when I was a kid," he said.

"Maybe that was before peanut butter was invented," I said.

"Hey, there," he said, "I'm not that old."

Mindy looked at Dad. "How old are you, Daddy?" she asked.

"A hundred and six," Dad said. "But I look young for my age."

"No," Mindy said, "you're not really."

"Of course I'm not," said Dad. "But Mom is." Then he laughed like crazy.

DECEMBER 4—WEDNESDAY

The winners of the class spelling bees were posted on the bulletin board. The other sixth-grade winners are Marcy Lipton and Steve Mayer.

On Friday morning we are going to have a spelling

bee in the auditorium for the championship of the school. The winner will represent the school in the district spelling bee.

Now I know I have no chance to win. Because Steve Mayer is a brain. He always writes words down on index cards he carries around and then he memorizes them. So how could I beat him?

I will do my best. What else can I do?

DECEMBER 5—THURSDAY

I am so mad I could spit.

Steve Mayer came over to where I was having lunch with Libby and Ned and he had his shadow, Billy Alston, alongside of him. "So you won your class spelling bee," he said to me. He had this smile on his face that I can't stand to look at. "Must be a very dumb class," he said in a sneery way.

"Buzz off, birdbrain," Libby said.

"*The Baseball Life of Johnny Bench,*" Steve said and he laughed. And when he laughed Billy Alston did too. "I just wanted to tell you something," Steve said. "You have no chance tomorrow. None, whatsoever." Then he and Billy walked off.

"Now I really have to win that spelling bee," I said. "Just so Steve Mayer doesn't."

"You'll win," Libby said.

"He's better than me," I said.

"How do you know?" said Libby. "He didn't win even the class spelling bee last year, did he? We were both in his class."

"Don't be afraid of him," Ned said.

"I'm not afraid of him," I said. "He just gets me so mad."

I am very nervous. I have been studying the spelling lists they gave me. But I know there will be words I've never even heard of or read before, and I will probably make a stupid mistake on one of them in front of the whole school.

DECEMBER 6—FRIDAY

I went to bed nervous and I woke up the same way.

I picked at my cereal and one slice of toast, then had a glass of milk. "Are you okay?" Dad asked me. "You look a little green around the gills."

"I'm fine," I said. "Just scared about the spelling bee."

"Loosen up," Dad said. "What's the worst thing that can happen?"

"I'll lose."

"Right. And what if you do? They won't shoot you, will they?"

"No."

"We'll all still love you, won't we?"

"I hope so," I said. "I really want to win. But there's this other kid who's so much smarter than I am."

"How do you know that?" Dad said. "Maybe this other guy will have a bad day. You can't go out there thinking you will lose, or you will. Just tell yourself, 'I'm the best there is.' And maybe you will be."

"I'm the best there is," I said.

It sounded good in my mind. But in my heart, I didn't believe it.

It was a clear sunny day and not too cold, so our classes lined up in the yard. Libby, Ned, and Dolf wished me good luck. "Beat that show-off," Libby said.

At the right time I went down to the auditorium. Miss

Pedersen checked off my name on a list. I said hello to Marcy Lipton and one of the fifth-graders I knew. Steve Mayer was sitting on one of the chairs down front on the stage. I walked over with Marcy and made sure she sat down next to Steve Mayer, because I sure didn't want to. "Good luck," Marcy said to me, and I wished her the same.

After a long delay while Mr. Guma got the microphone to work—it kept howling like it always does—we got started. My heart was beating very fast and my mouth was dry. "You are the best there is," I told myself, but it sounded false in my head.

Miss Pedersen got up and recited the rules, which we all knew by heart anyway. One by one, the six of us got introduced, and we stood up for a second while our classes applauded.

On the first round we all answered correctly, although I almost flubbed my word right then. It was *occurrence,* which was an easy one, but I paused before saying the second *r* because I wasn't really sure.

On the third round one of the fifth-graders went out. Then Marcy Lipton missed an easy one—*satellite*—and one of the other fifth-graders missed his word. Now there were only three of us left.

We went through five rounds of words without a mistake. I was starting to feel much better, especially when Steve Mayer hesitated for a long time on *quintessence,* which is a word I knew cold. I couldn't believe he didn't know how to spell that word.

We went through ten rounds after that. Nobody wanted to make a mistake, it looked like.

We went through three more rounds until the last fifth-grader, Charlie Liu, missed *molasses* by spelling it with two *l*'s. He sat down and there was only Steve Mayer and me left.

Miss Pedersen spelled out the rules from that point. While she was saying all that I glanced at Steve Mayer and he looked like I felt at breakfast—nervous and probably a little scared.

Because of the way we were standing, Steve Mayer went before me. We went through seven words each without a mistake. I heard Mr. Guma say "They may never miss" to Miss Pedersen. On the very next word Steve Mayer missed.

The word was *millennium.* Steve Mayer left out one of the *l*'s. All I had to do was spell that word right, get one more, and I'd be champ.

"M-i-l-l-e-n," I spelled, then I stopped. Was there one *n* in that word, or was it a double *n?* I tried to see it in my mind, but I couldn't. But it sounded like two *n*'s to me so I took a chance and spelled it that way, and, of course, I got it right.

"Correct," said Miss Pedersen. One more word to go. I looked at Libby and Ned and they had their mouths open. They were probably more nervous than I was. Because, and this is the amazing thing, I *knew* I was going to win then. I just knew I could spell any word that came next.

The word I spelled to win was *scalawag,* which was so easy I hesitated a long time looking for the trick in it. Then I spelled it out, taking my time, and when Miss Pedersen said "Right" my whole class jumped up and started cheering and clapping.

All the other class winners came up and shook my

hand. I looked into Steve Mayer's face as we shook hands. "Lucky," he said to me.

I just laughed.

DECEMBER 10—TUESDAY

Mom went to see Dr. Kliot today. At dinner she talked about it with Dad. The baby has turned around, or something like that. It means the kid is getting ready to be born.

"When is that going to be?" I asked.

"The first or second week in January," Mom said.

"Or any time before or after," Dad said. "Babies decide their own birthdays."

"Maybe you ought to get Mindy's crib down from the attic and set it up in our room," Mom said to Dad.

"Not my crib," Mindy said.

"Yes, your crib," Mom said. "The new baby will be so happy to know that he's sleeping in Mindy's old crib."

"That's my crib," Mindy said real loud, "not the new baby crib."

"Mindy, dear . . ." Mom began.

"NO NEW BABY IN MINDY'S CRIB!" Mindy screamed. Then she ran away from the table crying like a baby.

DECEMBER 11—WEDNESDAY

Mom took Mindy and me to the mall today after school. All the Christmas decorations were up and the mall looked beautiful. The music was Christmas carols and the stores were crowded.

Mindy made a big fuss about seeing Santa Claus, so we went to the department store. There was a long line of kids waiting to see Santa. Mindy behaved herself while we waited, mostly because she was working on a big lollipop with a chocolate center. "Now don't be afraid of Santa," Mom was telling Mindy, "and speak up really loud so he can hear you."

Finally it was Mindy's turn. She walked up to Santa and he put her up on his lap. "And what's your name, little girl?" Santa asked her.

"Mindy Marder."

"And how old are you?"

"Four years old," Mindy said. She wasn't scared of Santa like some of the younger kids were.

"And have you been a good little girl, Mindy?" Santa asked her.

Mindy shrugged. Then she asked Mom, "Have I been good?"

"Oh, yes," Mom said, smiling, "very good."

"Well, then," said Santa, "what would you like Santa to bring you for Christmas?"

"A beautiful G.E. frigerator, a Cabbage Patch doll, lots and lots of chocolate, a year's supply of Lemon Pledge, and a brand-new Ninety-Eight Olsmobile," she said.

Beside me, I heard Mom groan.

"That's some list," Santa said.

But Mindy wasn't finished. "Milk-Bone dog biscuits," she said, "a set of patio furniture, a fly-away vacation in London, and lots and lots of chocolate."

Santa looked at her, a funny look on his face. "Anything else?"

"Yes," said Mindy. "Don't send the new baby to my house."

DECEMBER 12—THURSDAY

Mom is very upset by what Mindy told Santa Claus. First of all, by the list of things she wanted for Christmas. "TV is turning her brains to jelly," Mom told Dad when Mindy was asleep. "That kid will watch every game show in creation."

"She likes the noise and the yelling and the sound effects," I said.

"I will put a stop to that," Mom said.

Good luck, is what I thought. It is very hard to stop Mindy from doing anything.

"But she doesn't want the new baby to come," I said. "That's even worse."

"Do you know why?" Dad asked.

"No," said Mom. "She just says 'No baby' when we talk about it. And here I thought she was all prepared and everything."

"I'll talk to her," Dad said.

"I wish you would," Mom said. "And you, too, Michael. Maybe she'll listen to you."

Well, dear diary, maybe Mindy will and maybe she won't. One thing I know about my sister: She has a weird little mind of her own.

DECEMBER 13—FRIDAY

Friday the thirteenth, beware!

I was aware all day long. And nothing bad happened.

But all the same I was looking out for ladders not to walk under and black cats crossing my path all the time.

And something that was even good happened.

Grandma called and said she would be here for Christmas!

Maybe my luck has really changed. Or I have.

DECEMBER 14—SATURDAY

Christmas is only a dozen days away and I haven't thought about it too much. But I better start thinking about it. I have to buy presents for Dad, Mom, Mindy, and Grandma. I have about $40 saved, which I hope is enough.

It has to be enough. That's all I have.

It's funny about presents. Mindy hardly plays with the expensive Etch-A-Sketch I bought for her birthday. But she is madly in love with that little $2.00 music box that plays "You Are My Sunshine." She lies around on the sofa in the living room, turning that crank handle and humming along with the tune, even while she is watching TV.

DECEMBER 15—SUNDAY

It was a cloudy day, but not too cold. I rode around the block on my bike with Mindy riding hers, and I got a chance to talk to her about the new baby. "Someday," I said, "there'll be three of us out here riding our bikes. You, me, and the new baby."

"No new baby," Mindy said. "Don't want it."

"But it's coming, Mindy."

"No," she said, "no new baby." And then she wheeled around and sped off toward the corner.

I caught up to her and we rode together down the sidewalk. "Mindy," I said, "could you tell me why you don't want the new baby?"

"*Mindy* is the baby," she said.

"No," I said. "Mindy is a big girl now who sleeps in a big-girl bed and rides a big-girl bike."

She looked at me like I was an idiot. "Mindy is the baby," she said again and rode off.

When Mindy was taking her nap I told Mom all about what Mindy said. Mom was standing in front of the big mirror on her closet door, looking at herself. "Like a camel upside down," she said, "that's what I look like."

"But Mindy doesn't want to stop being the baby around here," I said. "Don't you see, Mom? That's it."

"Classic," Mom said, "absolutely classic."

"So what are you going to do?" I asked.

Mom shrugged. "Suffer," she said.

"Besides that."

She turned sideways and looked at herself in the mirror again. "I will have to diet for three and a half years," she said.

"Mom," I said, "this is serious."

"Maybe I'll go dancing on the moon," Mom said with a dreamy look on her face. It was clear she wasn't paying any attention to me, so I walked out. I went into Mindy's room and looked at her. She was sleeping so sweetly on her side.

And her thumb was in her mouth!

Mindy hadn't sucked her thumb like that for at least a year. I ran back to tell Mom what I had just seen. Mom was taking little dance steps back and forth, looking at herself in the mirror. I knew she was in some kind of crazy mood, so I didn't even tell her.

Sometimes I think Dad and me are the only sane ones in the house.

DECEMBER 16—MONDAY

The last week of school before Christmas! Yayyy!

It is always an easy week, although some teachers give tests and act tough and talk about giving homework over the vacation. But they don't. I guess they are just trying to keep us working a little bit while our minds are running around the Christmas tree that's coming. I always have trouble getting something nice for Mom. So I asked Libby to come to the mall with me.

Libby is the best. If I ever had to pick somebody for a girlfriend, it would be her.

DECEMBER 17—TUESDAY

Mindy was crazy at breakfast today. "Want my high chair!" she yelled at Dad. "Want my high chair."

Her high chair is up in the attic with her crib and her playpen.

Dad just laughed at Mindy, which made her mad. She refused to sit down in her regular chair at the breakfast table. Dad just kept on smiling and put her bowl of cereal and her juice in the regular place.

And my crazy sister ate standing up!

I think we are in for trouble.

DECEMBER 18—WEDNESDAY

I have worked out a good Christmas list.

For Dad, a tie or a shirt.

For Mom, some nice piece of jewelry. As long as it doesn't cost more than $10.00.

For Mindy, some toy or game that is not advertised on TV.

For Grandma, a vegetarian something, maybe a cookbook.

I met Libby at her house right after school. We were very careful going to the mall, especially when we got near it. You could get killed in the parking lot very easily, because people are going crazy looking for a parking space it's so jammed.

I got a great orange and purple string of beads for Mom that Libby said was cool. It cost $12, but it was nice.

In the men's department I picked out a tie for Dad, but Libby said it was too ugly. So I looked for a shirt and they were all at least $15. I couldn't spend that much. "After-shave or cologne," Libby said, which I hadn't thought of at all. So that's what I bought for Dad.

Then we went to the toy store. I picked out a neat jack-in-the-box for Mindy. I hope she likes it.

By this time Libby and me were too tired to shop for Grandma. We had sodas in the hamburger place and rested our feet. Libby has almost $70 to spend this year. "From baby-sitting," she told me, "and my allowance. Also I am very cheap and never buy anything."

Since she was so rich, I let her pay for my soda.

DECEMBER 19—THURSDAY—
FIRST DAY OF WINTER

When I got home from school today Mom was stretched out on her bed with a wet rag on her forehead. "Your little sister refused to eat her lunch today," she told me. "She wanted me to feed her."

"More baby stuff," I said. "So what did you do?"

"Never mind," Mom said.

Mindy was in the living room watching a game show.

When this lady won a prize Mindy called it out right with the announcer: "A beautiful set of patio furniture!"

Then she put her thumb back in her mouth.

DECEMBER 20—FRIDAY

What a great day!

We had our class party in the afternoon, and Mr. Pangalos was so nice. Whoever said he was a tough guy was wrong. He has been terrific all year.

We had chips and stuff like that, and sodas that we got from the lunchroom. Then we had our grab bag. Carrie got the Daffy Duck pin that I put in. I got a ring that looks like a watermelon. I will give it to Mindy because it's so ugly.

Jimmy was weird all day long. He didn't pay attention to anything. When I talked to him he said, "Here I am on the 747, heading out over St. Louis."

"Hey," I said, "wake up."

"Look below and you can see the Gateway Arch," he said.

His plane for San Diego leaves at eight o'clock tonight. That's all he can think about now. He had a smile on his face that wouldn't quit.

Jimmy is such a funny guy. One of the nicest things about this year is that the two of us became friends.

We all piled out of school like wild Indians when the bell rang. The sky was gray and hanging low, and the weatherman said that snow is a possibility for tonight.

I don't think I'll feel so terrific until next Christmas.

DECEMBER 21—SATURDAY

I still had to get Grandma's present, so I walked down to Mostly Books on Cortelyou Road. I found a paperback book that had about a million recipes for making eggs. I got it gift wrapped in beautiful red foil Christmas paper.

I still had $2.00 left. I went into the candy store and looked around. Actually, I was a little ashamed of the cheap toy I had bought for Mindy. So I got a half pound of the chocolate nonpareils she likes so much.

I was sorry I was so nice to Mindy when I got home.

She was sitting in the living room in just her underpants, playing with this little squeaky mouse that is one of her bath toys. "Hey," I said to her, "what do you think you're doing?"

"Goo goo ga ga," she replied.

"Mindy," I said, "cut it out."

"Goo goo ga ga."

"Are you nuts?" I said to her.

"Mindy's the baby," she said.

This has got to stop.

DECEMBER 22—SUNDAY

Dad and Mom went off shopping for our presents this morning. They wouldn't exactly say that's what they were going off to do, but I knew it all the same.

I stayed home and watched Mindy. She was wearing her pj top and just underpants again and sucking her thumb. In about a week she has gone backward from a four-year-old kid to a baby. In a few more days she will probably be wearing a diaper.

Mom and Dad came back with three shopping bags

filled with wrapped stuff. Dad took the shopping bags upstairs to their room. It's Christmas presents, all right.

Grandma called later in the day to tell Dad when her flight was so he could pick her up at the airport. Dad was steamed when he got off the phone. Grandma is taking a late flight. She will be landing on Christmas Eve at about eight o'clock. "That will louse up our Christmas Eve," Dad said. "Your grandma has a mind of her own."

Later on Dad took me and we went off to buy our Christmas tree. A few wet snowflakes were coming down, but they weren't sticking to the ground. We get our tree from Mr. Norbert, who has his stand in the big supermarket parking lot every year.

We set up the tree in the corner of the living room. We will decorate it on Christmas Eve, like we always do. The last thing that goes on is this silver-foil star on top. Then Dad will light all the lights and Mom will begin putting all the presents under the tree.

And then it will really be Christmas.

DECEMBER 23—MONDAY

I slept really late this morning.

I was eating my cereal when Mindy came walking in with her old pacifier in her mouth. She was chewing on it like it was gum. Mom took one look and yelled, "Get that out of your mouth!"

Mindy paid no attention. She just walked out of the kitchen.

"Mindy, come back here!" Mom yelled, but she didn't.

Mom got up and walked out of the kitchen. In a few minutes I heard Mindy yell, then Mom came walking back with Mindy's pacifier in her hand. She threw it into the garbage pail.

A second later Mindy came in yelling, "Want my thingy! Want my rubber thingy!"

"You are too big and too grown-up for a pacifier," Mom said very calmly.

"Am not!" Mindy yelled. "I want it!"

Mom just ignored her.

In the afternoon I was up in my room wrapping presents for Mindy and Mom. I was thinking about Mindy. Being the baby was great for Mindy. It meant everyone paid special attention to her. No wonder she was scared of losing her babyness. Some perfect stranger was going to come to our house and take away Mindy's title of "baby."

Well, I thought, if Mom and Dad don't want to solve that problem, maybe Grandma would. She'd know what to do, for sure. And in the next second I knew what to do too.

Mindy was sitting on the couch in the living room watching TV. She had taken off her jeans again and was in her underpants. I sat down beside her. "Are you the baby?" I asked her.

"Yes," she said.

"Oh, that's too bad," I said. Then I waited.

"A set of china and glassware," Mindy said along with the announcer.

I just sat there. "Yes, it's really a shame you're the baby," I said.

"What's bad?" Mindy said.

"Well," I said, "you know that babies can't have chocolate, don't you?"

"Mindy can have chocolate," she said.

"Oh, no," I insisted, "if Mindy is the baby, Mindy can't have Santa bring her chocolates. And I know that Santa is planning on doing just that. Delicious chocolates, all for Mindy."

"What chocolate?"

"Nonpareils, your favorite kind. But if you're a baby—"

"Want my chocolate!" Mindy yelled.

"Sorry," I said. "Babies can't have chocolate."

"Want it!"

"Sorry," I said, getting up and walking away. "No chocolates for babies."

I went up to my room. In a few minutes Mindy was there. "Tell me about chocolate," she said, then put her thumb back in her mouth.

"Are you Mindy the big girl now?" I asked.

"Yes."

"No," I said. "Big girls wear jeans. And they don't suck their thumbs."

Mindy ran off. She came back in a flash, wearing her jeans, her thumb on her hand and not in her mouth.

So I spun a tall tale for Mindy while she was being a big girl and paying attention. I told her about the chocolate she was sure to get tomorrow—the package that was in my closet. And for good measure I told her how the new baby was going to get lots and lots of chocolate too. But since babies can't eat chocolate, and if Mindy was the big girl . . .

"Then Mindy eats the baby's chocolate," she said with a greedy look.

"Absolutely and positively," I said.

For the rest of the day Mindy wasn't the baby anymore. And if we keep her chocolate level up for a while, she may not be a baby again.

Fooling my sister was as easy as taking candy from a you-know-what.

DECEMBER 24—TUESDAY

After breakfast I went looking for Mom. She was up in her room, putting things into a little suitcase. "Are we going somewhere?" I asked.

"No," she said, "it's my hospital bag. Just getting things ready. Where's Mindy?"

"Watching *The Price Is Right.*"

"Not for long," Mom said with a grim look on her face.

In the afternoon I started to get things ready for our tree trimming tonight. We keep the lights and the ornaments in cardboard boxes in the garage. I brought them all in and put them under the tree.

Dad came home about three and we started trimming the tree because we have to go off and pick up Grandma at the airport later. He put the silver-foil star on top of the tree first, which he usually does last. "I'm getting smart in my old age," he said when I asked why. "It just makes more sense to do it this way."

"But it always looks so final when you put it on last, Dad. And we all applaud."

"Don't get sentimental on me," he said. He seemed a little annoyed, and I knew why. He didn't want to go out again to fetch Grandma.

A little later Mom came in and talked about going to Aunt Helene's for Christmas dinner tomorrow. We usually have it at our house and Helene and the boys come here, but Mom wasn't up to it now. "She's making goose," Mom told Dad.

"And it'll be lousy," Dad said. "Helene can hardly boil water."

"We'll be together," Mom said.

"More sentimental nonsense," Dad said. "Honestly, the way people get so teary-eyed about Christmas."

Mindy came running into the living room. "Snow, snow!" she yelled, all excited. "Look outside."

Sure enough, little white flakes were whirling through the air and sticking on the grass.

"Just what we need," Dad said. "I hope your grandma's plane gets here on time."

We had dinner a little early, then Dad came back into the kitchen with his car coat on. "Who's going to the airport?" he asked.

"Me," said Mindy, and I said I'd go too.

"Stay, Michael," Mom said. "You can keep me company and we can trim the tree some more."

So Dad and Mindy went off—she was being her big-girl self today—and I cleaned up the kitchen. Mom was organizing the ornaments in the living room. When I went in to help her she was stretching way up to put this little angel on the tree. All of a sudden she stopped, looked very startled, and ran off to the bathroom.

She came out in a few minutes and looked at me funny. "Guess what?" she said. "The baby is starting to tell me something."

"Like what?" I asked.

"Like, here I come, ready or not."

"Holy Toledo!" I said. "What should we do?"

Mom smiled. "Don't get excited," she said. "There's plenty of time." Then she said "Oof" in a funny way and put her hand in the small of her back. She kind of slid down into the club chair and her face got red. She breathed a little funny, like short pants with her mouth open.

"Are you okay?" I asked her. I was starting to get scared right then. I wished Dad was home.

"Well, now," Mom said. "I think it's beginning."

"Oh, no!" I said.

"Take it easy," Mom said. "There's still plenty of time. You and Mindy both took hours and hours to get born. But maybe I ought to call Dr. Kliot, just in case."

I helped Mom get up from the club chair and held on to her as we walked into the kitchen. Mom sat down on the step stool near the wall phone. She dialed the doctor and waited through a whole bunch of rings. "It's Christmas Eve," she said. "I hope his service is there." Then somebody must have picked up because she began talking into the phone. She said something like her water is broken and the pains had begun.

"Do you have pains?" I asked her when she'd hung up the phone.

"All normal and natural, Michael," she said. "Not to worry. But we'd better start timing them." She got up from the step stool and went to the kitchen table, then sat down in my chair, facing the clock over the sink. As soon as she did she said "Oof" again and sat up real straight. We both looked at the clock. The sweep second hand was on five and I watched it go around the dial. Less than three minutes later, Mom had another pain.

"Three minutes," I said as the phone rang.

"Right," Mom said, "three minutes."

I answered the phone and said hello.

"Henry? Your voice sounds funny," said a man's voice.

"This is Michael," I said, "Henry's at the airport."

"Oh," said the voice, "Sally's son. This is Dr. Kliot. How's your mom doing?"

"I don't know, Dr. Kliot," I said, and Mom got up and took the phone from me. She told the doctor the pains were three minutes apart. Then she listened for a while and said okay.

"Well," she said to me, "I'm taking a trip to the hospital. Dr. Kliot is meeting me there."

"How can you drive the car?" I asked.

"There are always taxis—oof," she said. It was another pain. Mom sat up real stiff on the step stool and did that funny breathing again. When it passed she told me to go upstairs and bring down her bag and her blue sneakers while she called a taxi. I ran off as fast as I could. When I came down with her things she was still on the telephone. "This is the worst night of the year to get a taxi," she said. She dialed another number.

I looked out the side window of the kitchen toward the streetlight. The snow had covered everything and the flakes were swirling in the light. I felt my heart beating as I listened to Mom pleading with somebody to send a cab right away. I was scared. I didn't want to be here. I wanted to be in bed, sleeping, then have Dad come in and tell me that now I had a new baby brother. "Oof," Mom said, and I turned around and she was hanging on to the step stool for dear life with another pain.

I ran over and took the telephone from Mom's hand. "Look, mister," I yelled into it, "my mom is having a baby and we need a taxi right now."

"Listen," a man said, "do you know what night this is? I have exactly three cabs working and they're all busy. Call the police, son. That's what I'd do."

I dialed 911.

"Take it easy," the policeman kept saying as I told him what was going on. I had to repeat my name and address twice for him. "I'll have a patrol car there in two minutes," the policeman said.

"It's okay, Mom," I said as I hung up the phone. "The police are going to give you a ride to the hospital."

"Good." She nodded. Her face looked white and sweaty. "My handbag!" she remembered suddenly. "It's on my dresser upstairs."

I ran up and got it and when I came down Mom was standing by the front-hall closet. I helped her into her coat, then remembered her suitcase and I ran into the kitchen to fetch it. Then I looked down. Mom was still wearing her slippers. I ran back and got her blue sneakers, and while Mom leaned against the closet door, I put them on her feet. Then I got my down jacket out of the closet and began to put it on. "Where do you think you're going?" Mom said.

"With you."

"You should stay here, Michael."

"No way," I said. "I'm not letting you go to the hospital alone."

I saw the police car pull up in front of the house. A tall policeman came out of it and started walking toward the house. "Let's go," I said, and opened the door. I had Mom's suitcase and her handbag. Mom leaned on my shoulder and we went outside into the falling snow.

The policeman drove very slowly because the roads were real slippery. The ride took about ten minutes, and when we pulled into the entrance a couple of men put Mom into a wheelchair and rolled her inside. I was right beside her.

A man with a clipboard came over and asked Mom's name and the name of her doctor. He said there were forms to be filled out. Then the elevator door opened and the men wheeled Mom inside. "All my ID is in my handbag, Michael," Mom said to me. I started to follow Mom, but the man with the clipboard stopped me. "You'll have to go to the admittance office," he told me, and I followed him down the hall.

I sat and waited in this tiny office with glass walls. After about half an hour a lady in a red sweater showed up.

She looked at me in a funny way. "You can't be the father?" she said.

"No," I said, "I'm the son."

The lady shrugged and put a form in the typewriter. Then she began asking me questions and typing when I gave her the answers. After a while I looked through the wallet in Mom's handbag to find her insurance card. Then the lady was finished. "Where's my mom?" I asked her.

"She's on the delivery floor, six," she said.

I took the handbag and suitcase with me and went to the elevator. Now I was getting worried about Dad. He was probably home already and trying to figure out where Mom and I had gone. I went on up to the sixth floor. When I got off I walked along this corridor and saw a room that was marked VISITOR'S LOUNGE. I went in and they had a telephone there.

Two men were sitting on chairs; one of them was asleep and the other guy was smoking.

I got a quarter out of Mom's wallet and dialed home. The phone rang about twenty times.

I sat down on a couch and put Mom's things beside me. The man who was awake looked at me. "Sixteen hours I've been here," he said. "It's our first baby."

The man stood up and stretched. "There's a coffee machine down the hall," he said to me. "Can I bring you a cup?"

"Thanks," I said, "but I'm not allowed to have coffee."

I watched the man leave, come back, and drink his cup of coffee. I told him why I was here with Mom instead of Dad. "Maybe you should call home again," the man suggested.

When I dialed home Dad picked up on the first ring. "Michael, where are you guys? We walked in and the house was deserted."

I told him we were in the hospital. "And the baby is coming, Dad."

Dad got real excited then. "I'll be there in two minutes," he said.

When I hung up I felt much better. I guess I hadn't realized how scared I was. I sat down in a chair and started shaking all over.

I didn't even know I'd been sleeping until I woke up and Dad was there beside me on the couch in the waiting room. "Merry Christmas," he said.

"What happened? What time is it?"

"It's just after midnight," Dad said. "You slept for about two hours."

"Wow," I said. "It's really Christmas Day. How did I get on the couch?"

"I carried you over from the chair," Dad said. "Just like I used to do when you were a baby."

I went to the bathroom and washed my face with cold water while Dad got Cokes for both of us. We stood at the window and drank them, looking out at the snow coming down and the streets without a car moving anywhere. It was really a silent night.

"You did just fine, Mike," Dad said. "Am I glad we didn't leave Mom alone tonight."

We sat down on the couch again and the time began to drag. I kept asking Dad what time it was and it was always only fifteen minutes when I thought it was at least an hour. "Does it always take this long?" I asked him.

"It seems to," he said. "You were born at three o'clock in the morning. It was a rainy night, I remember, when I took Mom to the hospital. We were both very, very nervous. You were our first baby."

"How about Mindy?"

"She was born just after eleven at night. I came home, woke you up, and told you you had a sister. You just looked at me with your sleepy face, said, 'Good,' and went right back to sleep."

"I don't remember that," I said.

We settled down to some more waiting. I managed to stay awake and looked through a magazine.

All of a sudden Dr. Kliot came in. He was smiling. "Henry," he said, "you have a beautiful son. Nine pounds, two ounces. And Sally is fine." He shook my dad's hand.

Dad turned and grabbed me in a big hug. Then he kissed my forehead. "A boy!" he said. He was really excited and happy.

I don't know why he was so excited. I always knew it would be a boy.

"We're cleaning up the baby now," Dr. Kliot said to Dad, "but if you'd like to see Sally . . ."

We followed Dr. Kliot down the hall to these closed swinging doors, where he stopped. "You're not allowed in here, Michael," he said.

"No way I'm not going to see my mom and my brother," I said.

Dr. Kliot looked at me. "Be very quiet," he said, "and don't say I let you come in here."

Mom was in a little room with a nurse by her, lying back on a bed. She smiled so wide when she saw Dad and me. We both kissed her. "Mitchell," she said, then she yawned. "I'm going to sleep for a week." Her eyes closed again and the nurse motioned for us to leave.

Dr. Kliot walked us farther along the hall to a glassed-in room. A lady doctor was holding a baby in her arms. She came over to the glass wall, pulled back the blanket the baby was wrapped in, and gave us a good look at Mitchell. He was so tiny! And his eyes were open and staring around and his face was all red and wrinkled. "Beautiful!" Dad said, just as I was thinking he looked very ugly.

"Let's go home, Mike," Dad said.

We had to dig the car out of the snow in the hospital parking lot. We started driving home really slowly, because the roads were icy and a lot of snow was on the ground.

"Hey," I said. "I just realized something. Mitchell's birthday is Christmas!"

"December twenty-fifth," Dad said.

"Right," I said. "And that means he always has to get

two presents. One for his birthday and one for Christmas."

"I guess so," Dad said.

"And no shortcuts. Two real presents every Christmas."

I guess my voice was getting loud, because Dad looked at me. "Do you realize what a wonderful gift this family just got?" He stopped the car at a red light, then reached over and grabbed me in a hug. "I hope he'll be like you, Mike," Dad said in a husky voice. Then he kissed me, and I could feel that he was crying. I hugged him, holding on tight, and I began to cry too. It was the first time in my life that I cried because I was so happy.

Dad pulled the car into the front of the driveway. It was four o'clock in the morning. When we went into the house Grandma was standing at the kitchen door. "A boy," Dad said, "and Sally is fine."

Grandma started crying and hugged Dad and then me. And then we were laughing together.

"Hey," I said, "Merry Christmas, everybody. It's Christmas!"

"The best Christmas I've ever had," Dad said. He looked at Grandma. "Let's all have breakfast. I could eat a horse."

We went into the kitchen and Grandma cooked eggs and toast. "Mitchell Marder," Grandma said as she sipped her tea, "what a beautiful name."

"Mitchell M. Marder," Dad said. "M. for Murgatroyd."

Grandma said we should all get to bed, but Dad said he was too excited to sleep. "Me, too," I said. "Let's finish trimming the tree."

So that's what we did. And then I got the presents

down from my closet and put them under the tree, and so did Dad and Grandma. When it was all done the sun was just coming up.

Mindy was sleeping all curled up in a ball, holding on to Horsie. I shook her awake and she looked up at me. "Merry Christmas, Mindy," I said to her. "And we have a new baby brother. His name is Mitchell."

"Where's the baby?" Mindy said.

"He's with Mom. In the hospital."

We got downstairs in a hurry. Mindy started ripping open her presents and I did the same. I got a whole bunch of them. A new sweater, gloves, a lot of books I wanted, and a video-game setup from Grandma. Dad and Mom got me a great digital watch that has the day and date on it and a stopwatch for timing things.

I took my last present upstairs with me, dear diary. And I set it aside as I wrote all this in you. It's the longest I ever wrote, and it just about fits in before the last page.

I think I grew up a lot this year, and I learned a lot of things. I am not the same kid who started writing in a diary on his birthday. I am a little older and a little smarter and I know some things I did not last year.

My last Christmas present came from Aunt Helene. It was wrapped in silver paper, and it came just in time.

It's a brand-new diary.

ROBERT KIMMEL SMITH never kept a diary. "But I remember everything that happened to me as a kid," he says, "including lots of things I'd rather forget." He is the author of *Jelly Belly* and *Chocolate Fever*. His most recent book for Delacorte Press was *The War with Grandpa*.

Robert Kimmel Smith lives in Brooklyn with his wife, Claire, and their two children. He lists his main occupations as writing, reading, cooking, and dieting.